Like a BOOK

Bette Hawkins

BELLA
B O O K S
2018

Bella Books, Inc.
P.O. Box 10543
Tallahassee, FL 32302

Printed in the United States of America on acid-free paper.

First Bella Books Edition 2018

Editor: Lauren Humphries-Brooks
Cover Designer: Judith Fellows

ISBN: 978-1-59493-603-6

Other Bella Books by Bette Hawkins

No More Pretending

Acknowledgments

Thanks to everyone at Bella Books, and thank you to my editor Lauren for her invaluable support and guidance.

About the Author

Bette lives and works in Melbourne with her long-term girlfriend and their two dogs. Bette enjoys playing the electric guitar, reading, and cooking. She is a movie buff and a lover of music. She can be found on Twitter @BetteHawkins17.

CHAPTER ONE

As she drifted awake, Trish resolved that she would treat today like it was the new beginning she desperately needed. When she threw her arms over her head to stretch, she looked up at the ceiling. She eyed the crack that ran from one corner of the room to another, and glumly dropped her arms. Why did she feel so tired before she had even left her bed? Summoning enthusiasm for a fresh start was easier said than done.

It was the house that made her feel like this. Trish had procrastinated about putting it on the market for the last few months. It was the home that she purchased with her ex-partner Katrina, and it was filled with so many memories that it was overwhelming. During the separation Katrina had practically given her the house. She only did it to alleviate her guilt over leaving, and Trish regretted agreeing to the deal almost as soon as it was made.

When Katrina moved out, Trish scrubbed the house until it was sparkling clean. In a businesslike fashion, she took down all the photos of the two of them and packed away any sentimental items. Still, every time she looked around she recalled all the choices that they made as a couple, from the paint colors to the bookshelves they built. Nothing could erase the ghost of their failed relationship.

Trish rose at last and tidied the covers before changing into her workout gear. The last six months had been bleak and lonely. The only thing that helped her to get through it was a devotion to routine and structure. She jogged around the streets in the crisp morning air for half an hour, then returned home to make the same green smoothie that she had for breakfast every day.

While she drank the smoothie, she sat on the back porch with her tablet to read the newspaper and check her email. There was an unread message from her sister Leigh. Leigh was very supportive, but she drove Trish nuts with her meddling. Leigh had just become engaged to a man she met online and was convinced that it would work for Trish too. She insisted that Trish download a dating app, which Trish deleted after a couple of weeks and one single date. Trish was horrified to discover that the woman she went out with had a husband and was just looking for another woman to experiment with.

Trish warily opened the email.

Hey lil sis,

Guess what, you know that girl I work with, Zoe? I always thought you two would get along, but she had that bitchy girlfriend who used to call her every five minutes. Well, turns out they've broken up so Zoe is single and ready to mingle. Can I give her your number?

Leigh xoxo

Trish sighed, and hit reply.

Dear Leigh,

This note is to inform you that not all lesbians are attracted to one another.

Kind regards,

Trish.

No matter how nice this random colleague was, Trish wouldn't be interested. She was nowhere near being ready for another relationship yet and didn't see why she should be.

The breakup with Katrina had been a huge blow to her. After eight years together, Trish had not seen it coming. They had been so committed to one another, tied together by the house and the car and the joint savings account. The two of them wore matching silver rings and regularly discussed plans to get married. They had problems, but Trish told herself that with enough work they could get through them. Then Katrina returned home from work one day and told Trish that she didn't love her anymore, and that was that. Trish powered down her tablet, wishing that she could get through a day where Katrina wasn't one of the first things she thought about.

Trish showered and dressed in the clothes she'd laid out the evening before: a gray dress, light scarf, and black cardigan. During the interview they hadn't mentioned what she should wear, but she reasoned that what she'd worn at the public library should be fine for the university library too. For work she liked to dress conservatively, though she was much more at home in jeans and T-shirts.

As she walked to the train station, Trish checked her watch, hoping that she'd planned the commute well enough. She lived in the leafy Melbourne suburb of Fairfield, and while it wasn't far from the city center, she didn't want to battle the peak hour traffic. She was going to miss being able to walk to work as she'd done in the past, but at least she could get some reading done on the train.

Her plan was thwarted when the carriage was too crowded to get a seat, and she was so hemmed in she couldn't get to her bag. Without the distraction of a book, she worried all the way to her stop. It had been a while since she'd started a new job.

Holt University was right in the heart of the Central Business District. The station was bustling with people, and Trish pushed past suited-up men to get to the escalators.

When she arrived, she had to check the campus map again to find her new workplace. It was a beautiful fall day and trees with turning leaves dotted the campus. Holt was one of the most prestigious universities in Melbourne, and the library was legendary. Her interview hadn't been in the library itself, so she couldn't wait for the chance to explore properly. When she finally got there, Trish paused to gawk up at the library. It was a huge structure, an impressive stone building split over five levels. The library was already open and she watched students scurrying into it. A kick of excitement overrode her nerves. She loved libraries—all of them.

From an early age, she had been a voracious reader, and as a young adult she had dreamed about becoming a writer. The practical side of her had won out, though, and she applied to study information and knowledge management, so that she could be qualified to work as a librarian. It may not be the most exciting career out there, and Katrina always said that she could be doing something more challenging, but Trish adored it. It meant being surrounded by stories all day long. She loved the quiet marked by the sound of turning pages, and she loved giving recommendations to anyone who asked. There was nothing like the feeling she got from guiding people toward some bit of information they needed and seeing their relief when they found it.

She pushed open the glass doors and walked across the marbled floor of the foyer. There was gorgeous artwork on the walls, and a reading room off to her right. Gazing around at the high ceilings and stacks of books, Trish approached the front desk.

"Can I help you?" the woman behind the counter asked. She was in her late fifties, with short salt-and-pepper hair. Trish was accustomed to being one of the younger librarians wherever she worked.

"Yes, thank you, I'm looking for Ms. Rose?"

"Yes?"

"Yes?" Trish asked.

"Yes, I'm Ms. Rose."

"Okay. I'm Trish. The new librarian? They told me when they called to offer the job to ask for you?"

"I see. If they had allowed me to join the interview panel as I requested I would have known whom I was expecting."

Trish pulled her shoulders back gamely. When women like Ms. Rose found a role they liked, they tended to stay and rule everyone else with an iron fist. If Trish could ingratiate herself with Ms. Rose, things between them would be fine.

"Hopefully you'll think they made the right choice."

Ms. Rose's eyes darted up and down the length of Trish from behind her glasses.

"I hope so. I'll be with you in a moment, I need to speak to the young lady behind you that's waiting for my attention."

"Oh." Trish peered back over her shoulder. The woman had heard the exchange; she gave Trish a sympathetic glance.

Trish stood to the side while Ms. Rose tried to locate a book the woman was asking for. The student looked older than college-age, perhaps in her mid- to late twenties. She had a striking profile, her black hair tied up in a loose ponytail. As she gestured, she exposed the lightly muscled arms underneath her oversized white T-shirt. She was tall, and there was something cat-like about the way she moved as she took the book between her hands.

The woman thanked Ms. Rose and then turned to the side, raising her eyebrows and grinning at Trish before walking away. Her skinny black jeans flattered the curve of her hips, and she wore heavy-looking black boots. A leather jacket was draped over her arm.

"Well." Ms. Rose looked at her with narrowed eyes. "I suppose I could start by showing you around."

Trish pursed her lips to chase the smile from her face.

"Thank you, I'd really appreciate that."

* * *

June's alarm buzzed once again and she hit the snooze button, then seized it and turned it off. The sun was streaming heavily through her curtains. June opened one eye, and then picked up her old digital alarm clock to pull it closer to her face. She'd been reading it right, it was already eight. Groggily sitting up, she rubbed her eyes, her mind already racing with the panic of work left undone.

She had worked late at the bar and then spent a couple of hours winding down before going to bed. She'd managed to grab a solid six hours of sleep, which was better than what she got a lot of nights. On weekends she allowed herself to sleep in past noon, but throughout the week she needed to knuckle down and write.

June treated working on her book as though it were another job. It wasn't good enough to chip away at it for half an hour here and there while the world buzzed around her at the kitchen table or in cafés. She had to be at the library for at least a few uninterrupted hours before going to work. When she wasn't making ends meet doing casual shifts as a barmaid, she was a tutor for an Australian literature class at the university. All these commitments didn't leave a lot of time for leisure, but she loved juggling them anyway.

June rolled out of bed and pulled on a robe, then padded out to the kitchen. Her roommate Ollie wasn't up yet. Ollie also worked in a bar, Sapphire, a place in the city center that stayed open until late. June worked at The Dickens, and unlike Sapphire there was no velvet rope and no bouncers. It was a cozy little place that drew an after-work crowd and some loyal regulars. June had been there for a couple of years and by now she knew the cocktail recipes and wine list like the back of her hand.

June yawned and started the coffee machine before looking around to see if there was anything to eat. She found a couple of pieces of whole meal bread on top of the fridge, and she toasted them to have dry with a mug of black coffee. While she was pouring a second cup Ollie stumbled blearily into the kitchen.

"Is that my shirt?"

Ollie looked down at himself and shrugged. He rubbed at his reddish-brown beard. The faded black Patti Smith shirt was tight across his chest.

"Sorry. I thought it was mine."

"You're such a liar. It looks better on you anyway. Late night?"

"Uh-huh. We were so busy and then we went out for beers after. I'm so happy I have the day off."

"Then what on earth are you doing out of bed? I wish I was still in bed."

"You're going to work on your book, I'm guessing?"

"Always."

The book could feel like a burden now and then. In her darker moments, when she was wrestling with a line of argument or wondering whether she had even chosen the right subject, she wished she could throw the whole thing away. Most of the time, however, she loved it. June was addicted to the feeling that came over her when she was on a writing bender. It could make the whole world disappear.

Ollie pulled a chair up to the table and June poured him a cup of coffee.

"How was your night, dear?" June asked.

Ollie took a mouthful of coffee, wincing at how strong she'd made it. "Delightful. Gerald asked me out, can you believe it?"

"The bouncer? Oh my. What a dark horse."

They had been roommates for years, and friends since high school. June still ribbed Ollie about how he'd gotten drunk on cheap wine and then told her he thought it was important that they start hanging out. He'd earnestly explained that he thought she was the only cool person in their whole year. The two of them had supported each other through everything, from coming out to breakups.

June quickly got herself ready, then packed her laptop into her bag before mounting her motorbike. Riding to the library cleared her head and helped her to get into the right frame of mind to work. The bike was cheaper to run than a car, which was the main reason she had it.

June parked her bike and kicked down the stand. There was a woman on the steps, staring up at the building. While June pulled off her helmet and jacket, she watched. Though she couldn't see the woman's face, June could admire the loveliness of her figure. The woman was a little shorter than her, with a subtle curviness. She had beautiful legs, her calves accentuated by the low heels she wore. June had the urge to call out something so that the woman would turn around and she could see what her face looked like.

June walked into the library behind her. The woman's hips swayed while she walked, taking her time, staring around the lobby. She hadn't been here before, June didn't think. Maybe she should offer to help her find what she was looking for. At the last minute, June realized that they were both headed for the front counter.

June hung back while the mystery woman spoke to Ms. Rose. She overheard that her name was Trish. June liked putting a name to her. Trish's voice was soft and deeper than she would have expected, giving the impression that Trish was the kind of serious woman that June had always been drawn to.

Ms. Rose was a bitter old crone but she could be sweet when she wanted to, and June had come to appreciate her efficiency. Right now, though, she was giving Trish a hard time. Trish handled Ms. Rose calmly and politely, like she'd clocked everything about Ms. Rose in a heartbeat.

When Trish turned around to walk past, June was finally able to see her face. If there was such a thing as a textbook definition of a sexy librarian, a picture of her would be an excellent illustration to go along with it. Trish had beautiful bone structure; well-drawn cheekbones and a delicate chin. Her honey-blond hair was scraped back into a bun. A couple of wisps of hair had escaped from it and were curling gently around her face. The hemline of her dress was modest, ending just below her knee, but the understated toughness in her voice hinted that she might be less demure than she appeared.

When June was walking away with the book safely in her hands she couldn't resist making a face at Trish, just to see her full red lips curl up in a smile. Trish adjusted her glasses and June saw that behind them, she had amazing blue-gray eyes. When they made eye contact, Trish's gaze was surprisingly direct. For just a second, June was sure that they were connecting in that unspoken way strangers did, and the rareness of encountering a woman who looked at her that way only made it more special. She smiled at the thought that she was going to be seeing Trish around the library now and then.

June left with her book to find a quiet corner. By now she knew where the best desks were—in the areas where students were least likely to congregate. A lot of the time, younger students came to the library to hang out with one another rather than study.

But today, the library, often dull, had become charged. June opened the book, spread out her notebook, and uncapped her pen. She took one last look over her shoulder to see if she could spy blond hair, and then she got to work.

CHAPTER TWO

Within the week, Trish was sure that her new job was the right fit. Each morning she bounced out of bed, ready to learn more. She was already dreaming about extra projects she could take on in the future, all the archiving and collection building she could do. It had been a long time since she had felt this excited about anything.

Although Ms. Rose had not warmed to her, the rest of Trish's colleagues were very welcoming. It was a large staff of librarians and assistants. Angela, one of the assistants, was a keen environmentalist who welcomed Trish by gifting her a reusable coffee cup. Chris, who worked in the audio-visual collection, spent a break lecturing her about the influence of New Wave cinema while everyone else groaned. They invited her to join them in their coffee runs and weekly group lunches. Trish sat listening happily as they talked and shared jokes, grateful for the way they included her.

It was nice to feel that she was connecting with her colleagues. Trish's social life suffered when she broke up with

Katrina, because some of their mutual friends chose Katrina in the split. Old friends had fallen away throughout the years, and she had realized far too late how isolated she had let herself become. Now that she was on her own, Trish longed to meet new people and to start having fun again.

The job was more demanding and busier than what she was used to, but she adapted to it quickly. When she had free time, Trish wandered through the stacks to take in the library and familiarize herself with it level by level. The collection of books and journals was huge, and much broader than any other she had worked with. Trish loved pulling out random volumes to see what they held. She flipped through the pages to examine the underlined passages and read the scribbled notes that could be from yesterday, or years before.

Though she loved the books, Trish enjoyed the human side of the work just as much. Trish was good at dealing with stressed students, she always had been, and now she had plenty of opportunities to practice her skills. She talked students down when they came to her panicking about overdue assignments. She provided a calming presence, helping them navigate the search systems and narrow down what they needed. There was a lanky, redheaded psychology student who came to her every day wanting to talk about the new angles he'd come up with for his research. Trish also met Beth, a brilliant student who was studying medicine. Trish and Beth worked on finding a good poetry collection, so that she could slow her mind when she was trying to sleep.

At night she went home and paced around, wondering if she could fix the house problem by doing more work on it. The new job brought into focus that she had been unsatisfied with a lot of things since the breakup. She had been sleepwalking through her life. It terrified her to think of how unhappy she had been even before that. Things hadn't been right when she and Katrina were still together, and she was only just beginning to face that fact.

Trish and Katrina stopped talking about the things that mattered long ago. Instead, it was as though they were performing a job together, running the household, doing tasks like hosting dinner parties and going out for Sunday morning coffee. Yet the dinner parties had been planned through a storm of disagreements about who to invite and what to serve. When they went for coffee, they would barely look at one another while Trish buried her head in a book and Katrina worked on her laptop.

The way they lived made Trish desperately lonely. She had wanted them to go to counselling to start working through their problems, but Katrina shook her off. When Katrina ended it, Trish wished that she had listened to her instincts more.

Trish learned too late that it was better to be alone than to waste your life with someone who wasn't right for you. She would never put herself through that again, no matter what.

Trish walked toward the entrance to the library, a cup of coffee from one of the kiosks inside Flinders Street station warming her hands. It was sunny this morning, despite the chill and she had reached work early, so she took a moment to sit on the steps and finish her drink. She looked out over the grounds at the lush grass, at the clusters of students lounging around before class. This was just the right place for her.

The loud roar of an engine made Trish turn to see a motorcycle pulling in to the carpark near the library. The bike was red and black, sleek, and quite small. As the person stepped off the bike, it became clear that the slim but shapely body belonged to a woman. When she pulled the helmet from her head, Trish recognized her from her first day at the library. There had been fleeting glimpses of her throughout the week, but this was the closest Trish had been to her since then.

The woman opened a storage case at the back of the bike and pulled out a backpack, arranging the strap over her shoulder. Her back was turned, and Trish's eyes dropped to study the woman's very nice rear end. Trish sipped at her coffee, feeling more than a little guilty that she was checking out a student. As a staff member at the university, for her to have any interest in a student would be highly inappropriate. But she could rationalize that the woman was older and had obviously come back to school late. It couldn't hurt to just look at her.

The woman walked over to the steps with the strap of her bike helmet dangling from her fingers. They made eye contact and the other woman's face broke into a smile. It was quite dazzling, how good looking she was. Her eyes were a clear green color, and she had a cleft in her chin. She was effortlessly cool in dark blue jeans and an oversized black knit sweater.

The boot-clad feet slowed as she walked closer to Trish.

"Good morning."

"Morning," Trish replied. She put her palm on the ground behind her and leaned back, the woman following the movement of her chest with her stare.

"You're a new librarian here, aren't you?"

"I am. My name's Trish," she said.

"Nice to meet you. I'm June."

June put out her hand and Trish reached up to shake it. June's fingers were warm and soft against her palm. They slowly released their grip on one another but neither of them shifted her gaze.

"It's nice to meet you too."

June finally broke eye contact and walked toward the library entrance.

"I guess I'll be seeing you around, Trish," she called over her shoulder.

Somehow June had made the innocuous sentence sound full of possibility. Trish tracked June with her eyes as she pushed open the library door, bumping her shoulder against the glass. It had been a long time since a woman had flirted with her like that, and she felt pleasure and remorse in equal amounts. She should be more careful. It wouldn't look good for her if anyone were to get the impression that she was encouraging June to act that way. Trish tried to fix the thought in her mind, but instead all she could focus on was the way June stared at her, and how high it made her feel.

The good mood that had ballooned inside her all morning threatened to pop when Trish walked into the breakroom. Ms.

Rose was the only other person there, and there was no choice but to try and make conversation with her. Trish had managed to avoid spending too much time around her so far.

"Hi, Ms. Rose."

Everyone called her that. Trish had no idea what Ms. Rose's first name was, and she suspected that she would never find out.

"Hello. I've just made a pot of tea if you'd like a cup."

"That would be great, thanks."

They sat at the table, Trish swirling a spoon in her cup. She glanced longingly at one of the magazines on the table.

"How are you finding it here?" Ms. Rose asked.

"It's been great. I'm enjoying it a lot. How long have you worked here?"

"Twenty-five years," Ms. Rose said. "And barely a day off in all that time."

"I can see why you would want to stay here. It's a fantastic job."

"It is."

Trish searched her mind for a neutral subject.

"Do you have children?"

"I do not. Mr. Rose passed away many years ago, not long after we were married. Before I could fall pregnant."

"I'm so sorry to hear that," Trish said. She should know better than to assume asking about children would be an easy subject, given how tired Trish had become of well-meaning enquiries since she'd reached her thirties. Expectations about things like kids and marriage could be destructive if you didn't follow the same path as most people did.

"Thanks. But it's all a very long time ago now. And you?"

"Oh no. I'm not married or anything. I live alone. Thank you for the tea, I should get back to work."

Trish made a mental note to be more careful about the type of questions she asked people. You never knew what someone's story might be. Trish had always been disinterested in getting to know Ms. Rose. If she'd known her history, Trish might have made more of an effort to be nice, and she definitely would have been more forgiving about her prickly ways.

Trish's problems were tiny in comparison to what Ms. Rose had been through. It made her ashamed to think about the way she had been wallowing about her split with Katrina. Trish was still young and healthy, and nothing tragic had happened. She and Katrina had just gone their separate ways, like people did all the time. It was okay to be sad about it, but why was she letting it rule her life?

June was in the zone, typing rapidly as her eyes flicked between her notes and the screen of her laptop. For a couple of days this week she had written haltingly, grinding out the sentences one by one. The best way she'd found to deal with writer's block was just to push through and wait it out, and it was finally working.

June knocked her pen off the desk with her elbow, looking down to watch it roll away before deciding to ignore it. A moment later the pen reappeared back on her desk, attached to fingers. June looked up. Trish was standing there, looking down at her. Trish withdrew her hand and continued on, pushing a cart loaded up with books toward a nearby shelf.

"Thank you," June said.

Trish looked back at her. "You're welcome."

Trish scanned the spines of the books on the shelf, searching for the right place to deposit the book she was holding. June's gaze followed the line of Trish's waist and hip, then dropped down to her legs underneath her blue dress. Biting her lip, June reluctantly looked back at her computer screen. The train of thought was gone.

June felt Trish's eyes on her.

"Are you working on an assignment right now?" Trish asked, her thumb running along the bottom of the book she held.

"Something like that. I'm writing a book," June said.

Trish whistled. "A book? That's a lot of work. Impressive. How's it going?"

"Slowly but surely. I'm getting a lot done today."

"Glad to hear it. Do you mind if I ask what it's about?"

"No, of course not," June said. There was a range of answers that she could give to that question. For students or close friends, June usually went into detail, but for casual enquiries she had a much shorter answer. Trish could be placed in a separate category. June wanted to impress her, to sound like she knew what she was talking about. But she knew literally nothing about Trish or what kind of opinions she might hold.

"It's nonfiction. An English literature thing," June explained.

"Fantastic. I thought about studying that myself once, I'm a big reader," Trish replied. "Well I am a librarian, after all, so one would assume so. What are you writing about?"

"Oh…it's 18th and 19th century, Western canon and all that stuff," June said.

"Really? Which authors?"

"A whole bunch, really, some of them obscure, some you'd definitely know."

June glanced back at her laptop, and Trish took a moment to respond.

"Well, all the best with that."

"Thank you. And thank you again for the pen."

"It's not a problem."

Trish turned back around and got back to her work. June wanted to say something else to try to explain her evasiveness or apologize, but the moment had passed.

Trish wheeled the cart over to the next shelf, her shoulders drawn up tightly. During their last interaction, June had been so different, and Trish wasn't sure what she had done to make her clam up. Most students she talked to were more than happy to talk about their work. She was writing a book and presumably sending it out into the world, so it was hard to understand why she should be so secretive, unless of course she just didn't want to talk to Trish. It had certainly seemed that way, given that June was barely looking at her.

This was exactly why she was so terrified by the prospect of dating again. It was too easy to misread signals. Trish hadn't fooled herself into thinking that this could lead anywhere but she still enjoyed June's attention. She looked forward to the harmless flirtation and to feeling desirable, something she hadn't experienced in a long time. When she noticed June sitting there with a lock of hair hanging over her forehead and her sleeves pushed up, she couldn't resist talking to her.

Trish glanced over at June, whose fingers had resumed tapping on the keyboard. To Trish's surprise she caught June's gaze slipping away from hers. Almost like she had been caught out.

CHAPTER THREE

It had been a long night at The Dickens. They were slammed because one of the regulars brought in a large group of his friends for his birthday. June mixed drinks and slid them across the bar in a steady stream, and she bantered with the patrons until closing time. After a long, soothing shower, it was time to relax. She was slumped down on the sofa and flicking between the channels on the TV, eating a bowl of cereal for dinner.

A key turned in the lock, and June hoped that Ollie hadn't invited his boyfriend over. Max was a nice guy, but she didn't feel like socializing right now. She was too busy ruminating on her conversation with Trish and regretting the way that she had shut it down. Ollie called out to her and then came into the room on his own. He was pulling his shoes and socks off, removing an article after every step or two.

"Good evening," he sighed, lying down on the couch and putting his legs over June's lap. "How was your day?"

June shrugged. "Busy night at work. You?"

"Same. How did the writing go this morning? Did you get anything done?"

"A little. I got interrupted, so not as much as I could have."

"Who interrupted you?"

"One of the librarians."

"That old biddy! Aren't librarians the ones who are supposed to go *ssshhhh*?" Ollie said, pressing a finger to his lips. "Why were they distracting you from your work?"

"Actually, this one is not old, nor is she a biddy."

Ollie kicked at her. "I know exactly what that face means. This librarian is a hottie."

June wished she hadn't mentioned it. She didn't know why she was so bothered by the awkwardness with Trish, especially when they barely knew one another. Maybe it had something to do with her bruised ego. June liked to believe that she was smoother than the way she'd acted today, and that she wasn't the type to get tongue-tied just because she was talking to an attractive woman.

"Is she into you as well? I love this. Picking up women at the library. I really must take my hat off to you."

"It's not like that. I've barely even spoken to her."

"Sometimes you don't need to. Words just get in the way sometimes. Do you get a vibe from her?"

"I'm not sure. Maybe a little something," June said. "Or maybe she's just been acting polite. I don't even know if she's into girls, she's kind of hard to read."

"Oh, come on. It's all in the eyes. You can look into someone's eyes and know if they want you or not. You know what I'm talking about."

June looked up at the ceiling, trying to not show her exasperation. It sounded like a recipe for delusional thinking. Regardless of how good a person might be at reading body language and facial expressions, nobody ever truly knows what anyone else is thinking.

June patted Ollie's foot. "Well, if you look into *my* eyes, you'll see I'm super tired. I'm going to bed."

* * *

Trish stifled a yawn and looked around at all the familiar faces, marked slightly by years. Trish and her sister were close enough in age that they had friends in common from high school. The two of them had been invited out to a brunch date with a big group. It was something they did every couple of years. They were seated around a large table, the twelve of them chatting in bunches of twos and threes.

Trish was sandwiched between two girls from Leigh's year, Katie and Lindsay. She regretted that she had been drawn into a conversation about a new fad diet that Katie had recently started. Katie had always been health conscious and, along with half of the table, arrived in her exercise gear. When Lindsay chimed in with some pertinent facts about kale, Trish watched her speak, remembering that she'd had a huge crush on her all through her first year of high school. It was funny to think of now, because Lindsay was very straight.

Trish was going over the rest of the day's to-do list in her head when Alison leaned over to talk. Trish had sat next to Alison in biology class throughout eleventh grade. They had kept in touch here and there throughout the years. She'd brought her toddler to brunch, and he was now sitting on her lap and reaching for Alison's fork.

"Trish, how's Katrina doing?" Alison asked, pulling his hand back and holding it.

Trish was midway through a sip of coffee, and she took a second to compose herself. "We broke up six months ago."

Though she had replied matter-of-factly, she still found herself on the receiving end of a sympathetic look.

Trish scrambled to wipe it from Alison's face. "It was for the best. It's been a good thing for me, it's given me a fresh start."

"That's good to hear. It's such a shame, though, you were such a beautiful couple."

Trish braced herself for Alison to start singing Katrina's praises, to talk about how smart and accomplished she was. Katrina had that effect on people, particularly on those who didn't know her intimately. Trish didn't have the patience to hear it today. Thankfully Alison picked up on her discomfort and moved on to asking Trish about her work, so she had the opportunity to talk about how much she liked her new job.

Finally, thankfully, the brunch ended. After everyone said their goodbyes, Trish drifted toward Leigh. They'd agreed to catch up after the gathering and go for a walk around the nearby park.

"How's the fiancé?" Trish asked, latching onto Leigh's favorite topic.

She liked Andrew. He was refreshingly different from the type of men that Leigh usually dated. He had a dry sense of humor, and he was warm and supportive of Leigh. He and Trish had hit it off immediately.

Leigh sighed, smiling. "He's fantastic. He's over having breakfast with his folks this morning. He said to say hi to you."

Leigh gestured toward the pond in the middle of the grounds and they sat down in front of it to watch ducks glide across the water.

"Well, tell him I said hello back."

"I will. How's the new job going? It sounded good from your texts."

"It's great. I love it, actually. I think being made redundant was one of those happy accidents. It's worked out well."

"I always said it would open things up for you. You were in one hell of a rut. And what's the dating situation like? Anyone interesting on the horizon?"

Trish picked up a rock and threw it toward the pond, hard enough that water splashed onto a duck's back. "Seriously? It took you all of two minutes to bring that up. We talked less than a week ago, how would I have found a girlfriend in the last few days? Since when have I operated like that?"

"Not a girlfriend, just…I don't know, it's a new job, with new people. I thought you might have met someone interesting," Leigh said.

"Leigh, we've been over this too many times. You're obsessed with the idea of me getting into a relationship. It's only been six months. And besides, there is absolutely no shame in being single."

"Of course, there's not! You know how much time I've spent on my own. I'm not saying you should find the love of your life right this minute, I just think you should get out there a little bit. Take an interest in people, get to know someone before you write them off."

Trish moved to lie back on the ground so that the sun warmed her face. It might be one of the last nice days they got, with winter fast approaching. Leigh did the same thing, and Trish played with the grass next to her, pulling it up from the earth.

"I do take an interest. I notice attractive women all the time. I don't think you understand the reality of my world, though. It's a smaller dating pool with them. I can't always assume that if I like someone the interest is going to be mutual."

"Oh please, sexuality has nothing to do with it. It's not that easy to meet a good man either."

"Come on. You know what I mean," Trish said. "The odds of me meeting someone are much smaller than yours have ever been. Basic statistics, most women are straight."

"You don't even try, though. I've seen you when we go out, you don't even notice when girls are hitting on you."

Trish couldn't answer at first. She ran a hand through her hair, watching the wind blow clouds across the sky. It wasn't the only time Leigh had said something like that, and she was pulling the idea out of thin air. Trish had never gotten a lot of interest from women. When she'd come out in her early twenties she had hoped that something would change, that she would be able to send out signals to get their attention. Yet they just didn't notice her, and she was more likely to be hit on by men.

"I'll have you know I actually did meet a woman at the library who I thought might be interested in me. She seemed cool, so I even tried to talk to her." Trish caught the way Leigh's head turned toward her. "So, I am not acting like a nun. I do try sometimes, it's just that it's not always reciprocated."

"Who is this lady?" Leigh asked.

"Nobody. Just a woman at the library. She's working on a book and comes to my library to work, to study, too, I guess. I probably shouldn't even be thinking about her like that. I mean, she's a little older than the rest of the students, I think, but she's still a student."

"Oh, who cares about that? You're not her teacher. What does she look like?"

Trish nudged Leigh with her shoulder. "You're so shallow. But yes, she's very attractive. Dark hair, pretty eyes. A bit of a bad girl thing going on that I didn't know that I liked until now. It doesn't matter, she's not interested in me in that way."

"How do you even know that for sure?"

"Just like I said, I tried to talk to her and she didn't seem interested. She shut me right down, actually. Maybe she thinks I'm creepy, the old librarian hitting on her," Trish said.

"Don't be ridiculous. You'd never come across as creepy. And don't just give up like that! If you think you saw something, then you're probably right. She might just be playing it cool. At the very least you need to sleep with someone. She might be down for it."

Images of June touching her raced through her mind and Trish cleared her throat. "Why is that so important?"

"Because you haven't been with anyone since Katrina, and you need to get it over and done with. The first one is weird, but you'll feel much better once you rip off that Band-Aid."

"I can't do that. I'm not going to just go out and sleep with someone just to tick a box. I'm especially not going to hook up with a woman I've met through work, it would be completely inappropriate. If I meet someone and if it happens it happens, until then I'm not going to force it."

Trish crossed her arms. Of course, she got lonely sometimes. She craved affection more than she could ever share with Leigh. Trish could acknowledge privately that she would like to get in touch with that part of herself again. She and Katrina had drifted apart a lot toward the end of their relationship, so it had been much longer than six months since she'd been intimate with anyone.

Leigh made it sound so easy, but Trish had never felt confident enough to meet a woman and fall into bed with them. It wasn't a moral objection, but casual encounters weren't something she was built for.

"Anyway," she said, finally changing the subject, "tell me about the reception venues you've been scouting. Anything promising?"

* * *

June stood in the waiting area for the bathroom, and carefully lowered herself down onto the seat into the corner. Maybe she should go to the hospital to get checked out. It didn't seem possible right now that she was all in one piece and that she was going to be okay.

Footsteps approached, clipping along on the floor. June glanced up, and there was the blond hair and lithe frame of the woman that she had been vaguely crushing on. Oh God. She barely knew Trish, and this certainly wasn't her finest hour.

"June? What's wrong?"

"I'm okay," June said. She was unable to keep the tremor from her voice.

"You look pale." Trish bent down to her. Even under the circumstances, June's blood rushed with the closeness. "Are you sick?"

"Nope, I just had a minor accident on the way here," June said. There was no point trying to deny that something had happened. Trish was looking at her too closely for that.

"A car accident? No wait, you ride a motorbike, don't you? I've seen you. You had an accident on your bike? Do you need help?"

"Thanks, but it was really nothing serious. The roads are wet, and some idiot cut me off. I had to slam on the brakes and the bike skidded away from me. I wasn't going very fast or it would have been much worse."

"That sounds like a close call. I'd be shaken up," Trish said. Her gaze moved up and down June's body, searching. "Are you sure you're okay? Are you in any pain?"

June had come down hard on her arm and her wrist was aching, but it didn't look like there was anything wrong with it. Most of the impact had been felt in her leg.

"My thigh is a little sore. But I wasn't going fast. It's probably just going to be a bit bruised. I mean, I play roller derby; it's not like I'm a stranger to getting knocked around. I should be made of tougher stuff than this."

"Roller derby? I'm not sure I know what that is," Trish said.

"It's a game, on skates. It can get pretty rough," June replied, wondering why she was babbling about her weekend sport. She wasn't usually one to make nervous chitchat. It must be the effects of the shock.

"Oh," Trish said. "That sounds interesting. Listen, have you checked yourself out yet, looked to see if you have any cuts or grazes or anything?"

Their eyes met. Trish was even more beautiful than June had first realized. She'd always been a sucker for a woman who wore glasses. Trish's frames were thick, and the classic almond shape of her eyes stood out beneath them. She really did have the most amazing cheekbones.

June stared down at her own jeans.

"You'll need to take them off," Trish said.

June's eyes widened.

"I meant you should go and do it in one of the stalls," Trish said, gesturing and biting her lips as though she was trying to not laugh.

June smiled. "Right. Of course."

June waved off Trish's hand as she tried to help her up and went to the nearest cubicle. June unzipped her pants, feeling exposed despite the wall between them. She eased her jeans down past her thighs. There was already a faint bruise. She touched the skin lightly and suddenly felt better. It was reassuring to get on her feet and walk around; she was certain now that she was going to be fine.

"How does it look?"

June worked at pulling her pants back up. "It's totally fine. It's going to be bruised, but it's not that bad. I didn't mean to worry you. Just a little freaked out. I should get to work now, get some writing done. I have a class later this morning."

"Don't be silly," Trish said, worry draining from her face as June exited the stall. "An accident like that would make anyone feel shaky. Maybe you should tell your tutor you're unwell?"

"Tutor? Oh, no, I am the tutor. I meant that I have to go and teach a class."

"Oh. You teach? Here at the university?"

"Yes, I do. I've graduated from here. I picked up the class when I was doing my thesis."

It hadn't occurred to June that Trish might think she was a student here, though now of course she could see that it was an obvious assumption. Was it June's imagination, or did Trish look pleased at the information?

"Well, then you can come to the staff lounge if you like. I'll get you some coffee or something, you can take a break and settle your nerves?" Trish said.

June walked over to the armchair to retrieve her backpack. "Thank you so much for your help but I'll be fine. Really. I should get to work."

They stood facing one another, Trish clasping her hands in front of her. June wondered if she was crazy to refuse the offer of hanging out with Trish for coffee, but she had been steadily losing time. As well as working on her book, she had a couple of things she needed to get ready for class. Maybe she should say something else, to make it clear that she would love to have coffee when she had more time.

She wondered what Trish's hair looked like when it was let down. While it was in that bun it was hard to tell how long it even was. She liked the way Trish looked with her glasses on, but she'd love to see her face when it wasn't obscured by anything. Trish cleared her throat and June realized that she had been staring.

"Thank you again," June said.

She nodded at Trish and walked past her, glancing again at her figure as she moved past.

CHAPTER FOUR

June stared out of the window of the carriage as the train flew past trees, fences, and houses. After the accident, she'd decided to take a couple of days out from the bike to gather her nerves. It had been minor, but it still shook her up enough to want a break. She bit her thumbnail and returned to her last encounter with Trish. Next time she went to the library, she would take something to Trish as a thank-you. Trish had been so kind; she had calmed her down just when June needed to be grounded.

Today, June had a meeting scheduled with Anne Adamowicz, a modernist literature professor at the university who had become a mentor to her. Anne was acting as an unofficial adviser on her book, and they needed to discuss the chapter that June had emailed to her the week before.

June knocked and pushed open the office door. The room was lined with bookcases, empty coffee mugs and papers littering the floor and windowsills. A framed black-and-white print of Virginia Woolf hung on the wall. Anne came around the desk to shake June's hand as she always did. She was barefoot, her toenails painted bright red, in contrast with her otherwise androgynous appearance.

"I like the polish," June said, nodding at Anne's feet.

"A friend's daughter. I let her practice on me. Sit," Anne said. "Tell me how you've been."

"Let's save the chitchat for when you've given me feedback, you know I can't sit here wondering what you're going to say."

"If you say so." Anne put the papers on the desk in between them. "I liked this chapter a lot, it's strong. I don't have too much to say, except that you can cut out these three paragraphs here, you're just repeating what you've already said. You've got a habit of doing that. You really need to watch it."

June winced. "I'll do my best."

"Don't be fragile. I'm helping make it better; that's what I'm here for."

"I know, I know, and I know I'm lucky you agreed to take the time and help me out with this. I'll take what I can get. I was actually thinking about asking someone from the library to help me out with resources too…do you know many of the staff?" June asked.

"Sure, I know some of them quite well."

"Do you know the new librarian, Trish?"

"I don't think so. Might have heard the name but we haven't met. Why do you ask?"

"Oh, um. No reason. So, how's your partner doing? Wasn't it coming up to your anniversary last time we talked?"

Anne twisted a simple gold band around her finger. June was touched by the way Anne looked right now, thoughts of her partner washing everything else away.

"It was, you're so sweet to remember. We had a great time. We went and stayed in a little cottage out in the mountains and drank too much champagne."

"That sounds amazing. How many years was it again?"

"Twenty-five, if you can believe it," Anne said.

"Wow. That's a damn long time. That's really something. Congratulations."

"I'm a lucky woman. We're very happy."

"What's your secret? I can't imagine spending that long with someone. How do you make that work?"

Anne leaned back in her chair and look up at the ceiling, as though they were back in class and the question deserved deep consideration.

"Honestly? There is no secret. You've just got to find the right person and then you've got to be willing to work at it. But Jodie and I will never run out of things to talk about, that's how it works the way it does."

"I've got to say, I really envy you. You've got this great relationship, you're a great teacher, you have all this brilliant work published. You know I want to be you when I grow up, don't you?"

"I don't worry about you at all, sweetheart. You're going to be fine."

June stood up and gathered her papers. "Thanks, Anne. Let's hope so."

* * *

Trish and Leigh were at their favorite diner, fueling up on protein after a class at the gym. Trish upended the ketchup bottle to pour a generous amount over her eggs. Leigh crinkled her nose up. "Ew."

Trish waved the bottle at her. "Don't judge me."

"You're gross."

"Shut it. Hey, guess what, I'm thinking about getting a cat," Trish said as she spooned the scrambled eggs onto her toast. She had spent a shameful amount of time the night before looking up cute pictures of kittens and watching funny cat videos. It had always been one of her favorite methods of cheering herself up. Trish loved animals, but she'd never had so much as a goldfish.

"Oh no, you're not. It would just give you another excuse to never go out," Leigh said. "You'd be like, I can't come out for a drink because I need to get home and feed little Fluffy. Eventually you'd end up with ten of them and they'd just crawl over you while you had your head stuck in a book. The only thing stopping you from becoming a crazy cat lady is the fact you don't actually have a cat yet."

"Stop it. It's just a cat, a bit of company and something to look after. I've wanted to get one for a long time, but you know I couldn't because Katrina was allergic. I think I should start doing the things I've always wanted to do. You should be encouraging me."

"Sure. Life is what happens to you when you're busy making other plans, and all that stuff. Speaking of major procrastinators, have you spoken to Dad lately?"

They laughed over their cups of coffee, gossiping about their parents. Trish was in the middle of a sentence about their mother's new obsession with golf when she noticed the way Leigh's gaze had caught on something behind her.

"Don't turn around," Leigh whispered.

"What, who is it?"

Trish watched Leigh's face, trying to figure out what was going on. Unable to resist having a peek, Trish looked back toward the front of the diner.

Her ex-partner stood by the counter with her arm draped over a woman's shoulder. It was completely Katrina's style to make it clear to the whole world that she was part of a couple. Sometimes Katrina had made Trish feel more like an ornament than a partner.

Katrina had changed her hairstyle, something she did often. The changes were usually dramatic. She now had a blunt fringe, her dark brown hair cut to just above her shoulders. She and her new girlfriend had rolled-up yoga mats under their arms, which was surprising given that Katrina had always said that yoga was "hippy-dippy nonsense."

Trish snapped her head back around. She guessed that her expression of shock must have mirrored Leigh's.

"Oh Jesus. I really don't want to talk to her. Can you see if they're getting coffee to go? Or are they being seated? We need to get out of here if they're going to be staying. I can't be in the same place as her." Trish covered her face with her hands.

"Trish!"

Trish jumped in her seat, then composed herself and forced a smile onto her face before she turned around.

Katrina strode toward her, and Trish stood to receive a hug.

Katrina had changed her shampoo. Her body felt strange against Trish's. Trish had a surge of longing, then an equally powerful sense of shame. When they pulled back from one another, Trish looked at the woman who was standing next to Katrina, a petite brunette with a trendy haircut.

Katrina and her girlfriend had put their yoga mats down like they weren't just stopping to say a quick hello. Katrina surveyed the table, checking out what Trish and her sister were eating.

"You didn't reply to my message, when I wished you a happy birthday. I was hoping you were okay," Katrina said.

Trish stuck her hands in her back pockets. "Oh, that's right, you did message me. I'm sorry, I've been a little busy. Thanks for that."

Katrina's companion was openly staring at Trish. Keeping one hand on Katrina's arm, the woman stuck out her other hand, and Trish shook it.

Katrina smiled. "This is my partner, Ash. Ash, this is Trish."

"I figured it was you," said Ash. "It is so nice to meet you Trish. I've been suggesting we have you over for dinner sometime."

Trish laughed, an awkward huff that came out without her meaning it to. How long had Katrina waited to replace her? In an instant, she was going backward, erasing the past couple of months and all the little ways that she had moved on.

"How have you been?" Katrina asked, with her head tilted.

"I'm great! I just started a new job, it's going really well."

"That's so good to hear. I'm glad for you. Well, we'd better keep moving. Our coffees must be ready. We've got a lot to do today. We're getting our new place all set up. Hey, Leigh."

"Hi and bye," Leigh said.

"It's lovely to see you," Trish said, looking between Katrina and her new girlfriend, a fake smile plastered on her face.

"We'll call you," Ash replied.

When they left, Leigh patted Trish's hand.

"Well, that was fast. She sure didn't waste any time. This is my *partner*, Ash." Leigh affected a posh tone to imitate Katrina, enunciating each word carefully as though she were giving a speech.

"I know! I can't believe it. They're moving in together already."

"That doesn't mean anything. That's what I'd call a rebound."

"Maybe. God, what if they were dating before we even broke up? Do you think that could be it? Maybe that's why she left."

"Stop it, you're making stuff up out of nowhere."

"Okay. I just think it's very fast. Don't you?"

"Of course it is, but it's a rebound thing, like I said. Why did she get on your case about that birthday message? I thought you told her you didn't want to be friends, that you didn't want to keep in contact and stuff?"

"Like she cares what I want. She thought I was being immature for not wanting to be friends after we broke up, that's what she said."

Trish pushed her plate out of the way and put her forehead on the table. When Leigh put her hand on Trish's back, she lifted her head again, looking over her shoulder to make sure they were really gone.

"You know what that is, just another control tactic, honey. You have every right to have whatever kind of relationship with her that you want, especially when she was the one who wanted to end the relationship in the first place. I hope you're not actually going to go over there for dinner if they follow through and ask you," Leigh said, sneering. She'd always made fun of Katrina's pompousness when it came to things like serving dinner. It was all about matching settings and starched napkins, recipes drawn from the latest celebrity chef.

"I don't know, maybe. I'm curious, I guess. Jesus, I'm in a rut, aren't I? And she knew it, it's like she could see it just by looking at me. I can't stand that pitying look she was giving me."

Leigh held up a finger, wiggling it back and forth. "Do *not* worry about what she thinks. God, I can't deal with her, I never could. You deserve so much better than that cold, stuck-up sorry excuse for a person."

"Tell me what you really think," Trish said.

"I never did that while you were together, and maybe I should have. I held my tongue for way too long. I can't do it anymore. I hate to see her making you feel bad about yourself. You're not even together anymore and she's still doing it to you."

"Can you blame me? Look at her, she's ready to move in with someone and I've gone on like, one date since she left me."

"There's no point making comparisons. Katrina's her, you're you, and you've always been totally different," Leigh said. "But to put it bluntly, yes, you're in a rut. You don't have to keep believing that you're only worth whatever she thought of you. You can change things any time, you know that, don't you?"

Trish shook her head. "It's not that simple. You don't know how much I wish it was."

Leigh sat staring back at her, and Trish could almost hear the gears in her brain turning. Leigh must get so sick of her complaining, but she never said anything about it. Leigh was her cheerleader, always encouraging Trish to make things better. Maybe Trish owed it to her to meet her in the middle.

Trish smacked her hand down on the table. "You know what, screw it, let's go out. I'm sick of sitting around the house feeling sorry for myself."

Leigh clapped her hands, her face brightening. "I can't believe you're finally going to take me up on that. You're on, sister. We're going to paint the town cherry red. Next Saturday night, it's happening."

* * *

June scanned the library. She didn't want the coffee to cool down before she could give it to Trish. On the day that they had introduced themselves, June noticed that Trish had a coffee cup by her side. After consulting with Ollie, she realized that buying flowers as a thank-you gesture was too much, even if that was what she really wanted to do. Coffee was more casual, but it was only a good idea if it wasn't handed over to Trish cold.

Finally, she spied Trish on her way back to one of the main counters. And she was alone, which was even better news.

"Good morning," June said.

Trish's eyes met hers, their bright gray-blue taking her breath away. "Good morning."

June put the coffee cup down on the counter. "I wasn't sure how you took it." June retrieved a couple of sugar packets from her pocket and laid them down next to the cup. "I wanted to say thanks for helping me the other day."

"Thank you, that's very kind of you. But I didn't really do anything." Trish smiled sweetly at her while she sipped the coffee.

"No, you did. You really calmed me down. I'm just glad it was you that found me in there and not anyone else."

"I was actually a little worried about you. I haven't seen you for a couple of days. I was hoping there wasn't something more serious that wasn't obvious at the time."

"Nope, I'm fine aside from that bruise and being a little stiff and sore. I took a break from coming in to write because I was meeting with a friend, she's helping me out with the book."

"This is good coffee."

"Glad you like it."

"How was your meeting?"

June rested her elbows on the counter. When she bought the coffee, there was no firm agenda in mind except to say thank you, but it was a nice bonus if Trish wanted to chat with her. She was still reluctant to talk about her writing, but she was okay with doing it if it kept the conversation going.

"It was good. She supervised my thesis, so it makes sense for to help me with expanding it. I'm writing about romantic friendships in history, especially in 18th- and 19th-century literature."

"Romantic friendships?" Trish said. Her slim, fine-boned hands moved around the coffee cup. She had very nice hands.

"There's this idea that women during that time were involved in friendships that were romantic but nonsexual. It's documented in letters, so we have access to a lot of sources where these women were passionately declaring their love for one another. And yet it's so commonly accepted that they weren't having sex with one another that they made a special name for it."

"I see," Trish said, smiling. "And your argument is?" Most people were either becoming skeptical, or began to look vaguely hostile by this point in the conversation.

"That the idea of the romantic friendship is a means of desexualizing women. The history has been written by men, mainly straight men. I'm arguing that it's a method of erasing same-sex desire because they can't imagine that it could be any different."

"Well, yes. It's hard to imagine people interpreting relationships that way if they were between a man and a woman. If what we're talking about were basically love letters."

"That's exactly right. Straight relationships must be sexual because that's what men and women do, but women aren't supposed to want one another. Women in general weren't supposed to be sexual unless they were receiving desire from a man. And you're right when you call them love letters, that's exactly how they read. This has all been explored before but it's a body of work I want to add to."

"Are you far along in the process?"

"I've been working on it for a couple of years, off and on. I've got a deal with a small press, but nobody will probably ever read it."

"I think it sounds very interesting. I'd want to read it."

"Thank you, that's so kind of you to say. It's important to me, probably because of what it represents more than anything. We're always trivialized, that's why it irks me. Of course, nobody can really know what went on in those relationships, only the two women involved, but I think there a lot of flawed assumptions."

"And so, what you're doing is taking back that history, rewriting it. Reclaiming it."

"Yes. That's exactly what I'm trying to do," June said.

"Well, then that's a great thing. Are you on schedule to finish it on time?"

"I will be if I keep writing at the same pace. Barring any further motorcycle accidents, of course."

Trish laughed so much it lit up her face.

"Anyway," June continued, "I didn't mean to go on so much about it. I hope I haven't bored you. What about you? Are you enjoying working here?"

"You're not talking too much at all. And yes, it's a great job."

"Where did you work before this?"

"Public library. I've mostly worked in public libraries, so this is a good change for me."

"I'm glad to hear it. They're lucky to have you here."

Trish looked surprised at the compliment, and June wondered if she had laid it on too thick, if she had come across as too eager. They fell silent and searched one another's faces. Trish broke eye contact first.

"Thanks again for the coffee. I should really get back to work."

"Of course. I'll see you later."

As June walked away, Trish's gaze was fixed to her back. There was a swagger in the way June moved, a loose confidence in her stride. It looked completely natural, like she wasn't trying to do it at all.

It satisfied Trish to find that her instincts about June had been right. June was attracted to women. There was surely too much personal investment in her subject for it to be any other way.

Trish had no intention of ever acting on the chemistry she could sense between them, a delicious buzz that hit her in just the right way. Just because she was starting to feel ready to move on from Katrina, it didn't mean that June was the kind of person she wanted to move on with. There was something a little bit wild about her that made Trish uncomfortable. It was the swagger, the motorbike, the way she dressed. It was evident

Like a Book 37

in everything about the way June walked and talked that she was a player.

June was sexy, but she wasn't a serious prospect, and Trish had never seen the point of dating if there was no chance of a lasting relationship. It was a waste of time. She had wasted enough of that precious resource.

The fact that June wasn't her type didn't mean that Trish couldn't enjoy a little harmless flirtation with her. Trish was only human after all, and she needed some excitement in her life.

CHAPTER FIVE

"Are you sure I'm not going to be a third wheel tonight?" Trish asked.

"If anyone's going to be a third wheel it will be Andrew. He totally invited himself. You don't mind him coming with us, do you?"

"Of course I don't mind! It'll be fun for us all to spend some time together. Do I look okay?"

Trish stood up and gestured down at her outfit. It had been such a long time since she'd been to a bar that she'd had to do some serious deliberating about what to wear. Eventually she had chosen tan boots, black jeans, and a black-and-white striped top. She'd pulled her hair back into a loose ponytail and was wearing contact lenses rather than her glasses.

"You look great," Leigh said.

Andrew walked in from the kitchen holding a bottle of wine, the stems of three glasses pinched between his fingers. "You both look stunning. Can I get you gals a drink?"

"So where are you taking me tonight?" Trish asked, taking a glass from him and holding it out so he could pour the sauvignon blanc into it.

"Andrew has a place in mind. It's in the city," Leigh said.

"You're not taking me to a meat market joint, are you? I don't know what Leigh's told you. But this is just about me getting out of the house, it's not a hook-up thing."

Andrew pushed his hand down slowly. "Calm down, lady. It's a great little place I go after work sometimes. This might surprise you, but I don't actually go to lesbian meat markets. In fact, I wouldn't know how to find one."

"Okay," Trish said. "But if you try to set me up with anyone I'm leaving."

Leigh grinned. "Duly noted. Andrew's got to work tomorrow, anyway. This is just going to be a quiet, relaxed night."

Immediately afterward, Leigh upended her glass and drained it.

One glass of wine turned into several, and by the time they got into a taxi Trish was more drunk than she had been in a long time. They'd spent hours joking about politics and movies and work. Being with Andrew made her feel like she had an older brother, something she'd always wanted when she was growing up. She was enjoying herself so much that it was hard to remember why she didn't get out of the house more often.

Andrew sat in the front seat of the cab next to the driver. As Trish stared out of the window, Leigh's hand touched hers.

"You're not getting the blues, are you sis?"

Trish turned to her. Was she so much of a wet blanket normally, that it made Leigh think that she couldn't cope with a night out? Perhaps Leigh's concern wasn't misplaced. There had been a lot of times since the end of her relationship that Trish had grown melancholy out of nowhere and ended up crying on Leigh's shoulder.

"Not at all. I was just thinking about how fun this is. Thank you for taking me out."

"Yay."

They spilled out of the cab and onto the busy city street. It was full of people quickly making their way somewhere else or leaning against buildings to smoke cigarettes.

"Where is this place?" Trish asked.

"Down there," Andrew said, pointing to a neon sign.

They descended the stairs and Trish found that it was the kind of quiet place that she'd hoped for. It was dimly lit, with booths lining the walls. Andrew pointed to the only empty one and they slid onto the leather seats.

"I'll get us a round of drinks. Wine for everybody?"

When he walked up to the bar, Trish checked out the brightly lit shelves full of bottles, and the people serving drinks behind it.

For a moment, she thought that the barmaid might only look like June, but after a second glance she knew for sure that it was her. June wore a crisp button-down white shirt, and her hair was tied into a sleek ponytail. She looked cool and comfortable behind the bar, neatly handling a silver cocktail shaker.

"What is it with running into people I know when I'm with you?" Trish said.

"Why? It's not Katrina again, is it?" Leigh said as she looked around. "I'm just about drunk enough to take her on."

"See that woman over there behind the bar? She comes in to the library all the time."

"Is that the woman you were telling me about? The one you like?" Leigh gave June an appraising once-over and nodded. "She's very attractive. Quite the tall drink of water. Aren't you going to go and say hello?"

"I don't think so. Maybe we should go…"

"We just got here! You're such a baby, wanting to run away."

"Okay, okay," Trish replied.

Trish watched as Andrew got to the front of the short line. Trish envied the steady eye June fixed him with as she served him. She wished that she'd gone to order the drinks, even if she was too shy to go and talk to June. When Andrew turned to walk back to them, he was grinning.

"Guess who just got drinks on the house! I guess all these years of coming here have finally paid off. I didn't think she'd ever noticed that I'm a regular, she's never bought me a round like that before."

Leigh's eyebrows shot up. "Honey, I'm sorry to tell you this but I don't think the freebies were because of you. That barmaid and my sister are hot for one another."

Andrew whipped back around to look at June. "Oh wow. Good for you, Trish. She's very cool. I like her. And her mixing skills are superb."

"Stop it," said Trish. "I know why she did it, it's just because I helped her out with something. By the way I'm not *hot* for her, I just find her mildly interesting."

"Yeah, you're mildly interested in having sex with her. You've been drooling over her since you realized she was here," Leigh said, laughing at her own joke.

Andrew giggled into his glass of wine. "Yeah, I bet you *helped* her with a lot of things."

"You're both being idiots," Trish said.

Trish slipped out of the booth. It would be rude to not go and thank June for the drinks, and she had always prided herself on having good manners. It was no big deal; she would only need to speak to her for a second.

June was serving the person directly in front of her, but she threw a quick smile at Trish. When it was Trish's turn, she bent over the bar, trying to make herself heard. June leaned forward, too, looking at Trish intently. The collar of her shirt was open, and there was smooth skin underneath.

"You didn't have to do that," Trish said. "You already bought me coffee. Here, take this."

Trish pushed a couple of notes across the bar. June's hand pressed on top of hers, and Trish's skin tingled when June gently pushed her hand back. Trish didn't take her hand away, and June's rested on hers for a few moments.

June smiled. "Just let me get this round, it's no problem. Are you having a nice night?"

"Thank you. And yes, I am. I didn't know that you worked here?"

"A girl has got to pay the bills somehow. I only teach one class, and obscure little books like mine are never going to pay much."

Trish glanced at the woman who was standing impatiently beside her, waiting to order a drink. "Anyway, I just wanted to say thanks."

"No worries. That your boyfriend?" June asked.

"Who, Andrew? Oh no. He's my brother-in-law. Or, he will be soon."

June acknowledged the statement with a cool nod, like she already knew Trish was going to say no. "If you're going to be here a while I get off in a couple of hours. Maybe we could have a drink?"

Trish's eyes cut across to the woman, who was now openly glaring at them. It wasn't a good idea. Trish was more than tipsy, she knew June from work and would have to see her there again. In a few more drinks she might be in a condition to make a fool of herself.

"I don't know…"

"Don't feel obligated, if you don't want to it's all good," June said with a smile, finally turning to ask the woman what she would like. She turned up her smile for the woman, charming forgiveness from her.

Trish went back to the table. "So, Andrew, Leigh mentioned you had to work tomorrow, how's it all going?" she said. Andrew smirked at Leigh, but he still answered Trish's question.

As he spoke, Trish thought about June's invitation. She couldn't sit still, keyed up from the tension humming between them, but it was possible that she was being presumptuous. Maybe June was just being friendly, and it seemed likely that she was flirtatious with a lot of different people.

Trish tried to remember the last time she had done anything impulsive. It depressed her that her mind was so blank. She had so few people in her life these days, because she was just too guarded for her own good.

The three of them had another couple of drinks each. Trish refused to go back to the bar, despite Leigh's prodding, but she never lost her intense awareness of June's presence, often catching her out of the corner of her eye. And whenever their eyes met, Trish's heart beat faster.

"I should be getting home," Andrew finally said, sighing. "Work is going to hurt tomorrow."

"I'm ready to head off too," Leigh agreed.

"Thanks, you guys. I've had a great time. I think I'm going to stay a bit longer, so I can catch up with June once she's done."

Leigh gaped at her and Trish held up a finger to signal that she didn't want to hear a word about it.

Leigh threw up her hands and kissed her goodbye on the cheek. "Okay, okay, just call me tomorrow. And be safe, don't go walking around the city by yourself."

When they were gone, Trish took her phone from her handbag and stared at the screen blankly. She tapped her foot under the table as she tried to fight the panic that had worked its way up from underneath the alcohol. It was stupid of her to stay here when she hadn't even talked to June again to say she'd changed her mind. Maybe June didn't even want to go anymore, maybe she had gone ahead and planned something else.

Trish looked over at June, who was shrugging on her jacket and picking up her backpack. When they made eye contact, June nodded at her, and Trish let out a breath she didn't know she was holding. They met in the middle, June leaning in again to make herself heard over the conversations around them.

"Do you mind if we go somewhere else? I kind of like to get out of here as soon as I've finished work."

"Absolutely."

Trish followed June up the stairs, watching the subtle swaying of June's hips. It was surreal; she had never imagined that it was going to wind up like this.

They faced one another while June pulled the strap of her bag against her shoulder. She looked around the street at the drunken revelers.

"You know, I'm not sure about that drink. Actually, I'm sort of hungry. What do you think about getting something to eat instead?"

"I could eat."

"Cool. There are a lot of great places in Chinatown that'll still be open."

June led the way as they walked through the streets. Trish was rarely out so late at night, but she loved the energy of the city. She felt buoyed by the backdrop of the bright lights against the dark sky. There were still people everywhere. The two of them talked now and then as they made their way, Trish asking about how June's shift had been.

As they passed through the gate of Chinatown, Trish touched one of the red posts and looked up at the arched golden roof. She'd come here all the time when she was a student, when she and her friends sought out the cheapest places to eat. They pulled tricks like leaving a single steamed bun on the table as though they were still dining, so that they could stay and drink without being asked to leave. Trish smiled when they passed a karaoke bar, remembering how many times she and Leigh had stumbled up those stairs.

June stopped outside a restaurant with faded red Chinese script along the wall. There were pictures in the window of dishes, and June scanned it for a moment.

"How do you feel about dumplings?" June asked.

The restaurant was busy, and they were seated on the end of a shared table. They were so close that Trish had to move her legs so that their feet wouldn't brush.

"So, that girl that was with you, that was your sister?" June asked. "She looks a lot like you."

"That's right. Leigh, my big sister."

"She's very pretty. And what had you all been up to tonight?" June picked up the menu and started to scan it while she spoke.

Trish had caught that the compliment about Leigh's looks was for her, too, and she shifted in her chair. "We had a few drinks at their place. Leigh's been bugging me to go out for a long time."

"Really? You're not so into going out?"

"It's been fun tonight, but no, not usually. I was in a relationship for a long time and she wasn't that big on nightlife, either, so guess I turned into a bit of a homebody."

June quickly glanced up at her and then down again at the menu. "How long were the two of you together?"

"Eight years."

"That's a long time. I'm sorry, a separation after that long must be rough."

"Thanks. It was difficult, but I'm fine now."

They ordered dumplings, spring onion pancakes, and a plate of pumpkin cakes. Trish looked around the table, at the groups of people chattering and laughing. There was a good mood in here tonight, a festive atmosphere, and she liked that she was a part of it for once.

"So, what made you want to be a librarian?" June asked, propping her hand under her chin.

"I've just always loved being around books. I explored a couple of things but I'm glad that I went down this path. Especially now that I like this job so much. And what about you, why did you choose literature to study?"

"Same as you. Books and reading have always been a passion of mine. Reading's like breathing to me, a daily need. Only I don't get as much time to do it as I'd like right now."

Trish played with the menu under June's steady gaze, opening and closing it though they'd already ordered. When she moved, her leg bumped up against June's. "And your book topic? Why that in particular? Was it something that you'd been thinking about for a while?"

"Sure. I first heard about the idea of romantic friendships as an undergrad. The idea was taught to us like it was a fact, no critical thought about it, and that always stuck in my mind."

"I can see why. Times have changed, we should be looking back at that stuff with a different lens now."

"I completely agree."

"But I mean, there must be…" Trish paused when the waiter laid their plates on the table. She picked up chopsticks, positioning them between her fingers before she continued. "There must have been cases where those women really didn't intend for their letters to be read in that way. There's so many different types of relationships. So many gray areas sometimes."

June poured chili sauce into a bowl and offered it to Trish, who waved it away.

"Yes, but even if they didn't intend it to sound that way, it doesn't mean those women didn't have desire for one another."

"I suppose. Desire isn't always acted upon, though. I think people can be friends and be attracted to one another, but not want to go there. There's something kind of nice about the idea of it, don't you think? I think a lot of people in general, men too, would like to be more demonstrative in their relationships. They'd like to be able to cuddle or hold hands, be more open with one another."

June shrugged. "Okay. I guess some people feel like that. My biggest problem though is the idea that women didn't know what they wanted because homosexuality wasn't viewed like it is now. Women have been figuring out how to have sex with one another since the dawn of time. It's natural. There's nothing new about it."

"Of course," Trish said, clearing her throat.

"That's interesting, though, that you think it's a nice idea. It's weird, that's something I hadn't even considered. That it could be an attractive prospect."

"It's a great topic. Maybe you'd even let me read it one day?"

June shrugged, but looked pleased in her low-key way. "If you wanted to read it, of course you could."

Trish bit into the last remaining dish, the soft center of the pumpkin cake sweet on her tongue. June picked up the water jug and refilled each of their glasses, smiling when Trish thanked her.

When it was time to settle the check, Trish reached into her handbag, but June quickly laid her card down.

"This is on me," June said.

"No, come on. I'd like to contribute."

"You can get it next time."

While June was taking care of it, chatting with the waiter, Trish's thoughts lingered on the concept of romantic friendships. With some relationships there was that spark, a frisson that might never be named. Ambiguity could be appealing, and tonight was a fine example of that. She and June were just acquaintances who'd bumped into one another and shared a friendly meal, yet Trish had spent most of the last hour feeling like she was on the best first date she'd ever had.

The waiter left, and June turned to her. "Shall we?"

They stepped outside and Trish pulled her jacket closer against the cold.

"I should get a cab. It's getting late. Thanks for having dinner with me, that was fun," Trish said.

"Thank you for sticking around." June put her hand on Trish's shoulder for a moment before dropping it back to her side. Trish crossed her arms, staring down at the ground and stepping back a fraction.

When she glanced up at June, she was adjusting the strap of her backpack and looking down at the ground herself, and Trish knew that she'd gotten the message. It was embarrassing to realize just how scared she was that June might try to kiss her. It wasn't that she wasn't attracted to June, but still the thought terrified her.

She wasn't ready.

"Listen, can I ask, would you like to hang out again sometime soon?" June asked.

"Sure. As friends?"

"Is that what you want?" June said.

"I think so. Yes."

June looked back at her, and Trish could read the trace of regret in her eyes beyond her smile.

"Okay. Fair enough. I'll see you next week at the library. Thanks again for the evening."

While she spoke, June raised her hand to hail a cab that was coming toward them. When it pulled over she opened the door for Trish, and turned to her. Trish hesitated, but then said good night and got into the taxi. As she slid down into the seat they locked eyes.

June shut the door for her. Trish leaned forward to give the driver the address, and when she moved back into the seat, June was still looking at her through the window. She waved, and June waved back at her.

As they drove away, Trish had to remind herself that it had been her choice to leave.

CHAPTER SIX

Trish had so much energy today. She'd slept in, then gone for a brisk walk. Her neighbor Eamonn was out walking his friendly German shepherd, Tucker. Though she usually passed by with a quick hello, she stopped and bent down to scratch Tucker behind his ears.

Last night, she'd caught a glimpse of what her life could be like if she opened herself up. June's easy spontaneity inspired her. Trish would never think to propose a midnight dinner with a near stranger, and Trish figured that she could learn something from the way that June lived her life.

Trish's Sundays were usually spent cooking and cleaning, full of chores that would help her to get everything ready for the week. That routine didn't feel like it fit today, so she folded yesterday's edition of *The Saturday Paper* into her handbag and walked around the corner to Gina's Place. Settling into a chair at an outdoor table, Trish realized she hadn't been here since the break-up. She ordered a long black and a croissant for breakfast, peeling off the soft buttery layers as she read the paper.

Trish turned to the crossword but found herself daydreaming about when she might see June again. There was a dynamic between them that Trish wasn't used to, a strange mixture of safety and danger. Their interactions were laced with a desire that she knew she would never act upon, but that didn't mean she couldn't just enjoy it.

When June had told her that she was a tutor at Holt and not a student, Trish was more than a little relieved. She would never do anything inappropriate, and that included violating her sense of ethics. From a young age, Trish's feminist mother had drummed into her that relationships based on power imbalances were not okay. It meant that she'd always been hypersensitive about such things, and she'd never liked seeing people being taken advantage of. The idea of being attracted to a student horrified her, but now she could enjoy her feelings with no guilt.

For the rest of the day, June was never far from Trish's thoughts. During dinner, June had dropped into conversation that she'd be writing at the library on Monday. So as she was getting ready for work, Trish spent a lot of time choosing her outfit. There was a top at the back of her closet that she hadn't worn before and she pulled it out to examine it, deciding that it was time that it finally saw the light of day. The silk blouse wasn't too different from what she'd typically wear, but the way it was cut accentuated her shape. Trish began pulling her hair up into a bun but let it drop down. She brushed it so that the waves fell over her shoulders.

At the beginning of her shift, Trish was busy repairing damaged books. When she was done, she made her way to the second floor, to the cubicles by the stacks where she knew June liked to work. She found June sitting in a corner desk, hunched over her laptop. Trish was reluctant to interrupt her while she worked, so she only lightly touched June's back as she walked past. When June raised her head, she quickly looked Trish up and down, her gaze running up to Trish's hair.

"Morning," Trish whispered.

"Hey," June replied. "Your hair looks so good like that."

"Thank you."

Trish went to the front loans counter and began to scan books, her hands shaking. She wanted to laugh at herself for having such an extreme reaction to the compliment. There was an intensity in the way that June looked at her that threw her, but it didn't feel bad.

Trish did her best to lose herself in work, going through the returned books pile to scan them back in. Angela came over to help out.

"What did you do on the weekend?" Angela asked.

"Huh?" Trish thought she'd seen June walking toward the doors, but it was only someone wearing similar clothes.

"Just asking how your weekend was?" Angela repeated.

"Oh, it was good. You?"

Trish checked her watch, seeing that the morning had flown, and it was time for her lunch break. She'd forgotten to bring a salad like she usually would, so instead she collected her handbag from the staff room. As she was going along her usual path to the front door, June was right ahead of her.

"Hey. Are you heading off for the day?" Trish asked, tapping her on the shoulder. June turned to look at her, smiling.

"Yep, I have to get to work. I'm just going to get some lunch before I go in. What are you doing right now?"

"I was going to get lunch myself. I don't suppose you'd want to get something together?"

"Sure. There's a little Vietnamese bakery just off campus that I was on my way to, want to join me?"

"Of course."

They walked so close to one another that Trish's handbag bumped into June.

"Sorry about that. You seem to know the city so well. You grew up in Melbourne?" Trish said.

"No, actually, we moved here when I was seventeen. From Queensland."

"Really? I wouldn't have picked you as a Queenslander."

June laughed. "Are you talking about my accent? I've dropped it a little."

She pointed toward the bakery, which had a line out of the door. They joined the end and ordered, then took rolls packaged in white paper bags to the tables outside.

When Trish bit into her banh mi she looked down at it, groaning. The fresh roll was stuffed with crisp vegetables and tender pork. It was perfect.

"How do you know about all the good food places? It's like a special power you have there."

June had waited while Trish lifted the roll to her mouth. After a few moments, she picked up her own and bit into it. "I like good food. My mother's a chef. She raised me to appreciate eating as being about more than getting fuel. She was always getting me to try different things, experiment with different flavors."

"Well, I'm very happy for you to pass that along. This is delicious."

Trish wiped some sauce from the corner of her mouth. Eating in front of someone you were attracted to wasn't an easy thing to do gracefully. She couldn't remember having this problem with Katrina, even at the beginning of their relationship. "So, you said you love reading. Who are your favorite authors?"

"Hmm. That changes depending on what day you ask me, but I do love Joan Didion. I like Nabokov, Dostoevsky, Faulkner. Lots of stuff, really."

"Whew, I'm a little intimidated."

"Who do you like?"

"I'm a Didion fan myself actually. And Patricia Highsmith, I really like her too. James Baldwin."

"So, you're no slouch yourself. Hey, there's something I need to ask you," June said. "If you don't mind."

Trish wiped her fingers on her napkin and folded her hands in her lap. June was looking at her in a way that suggested this was something serious.

"Go ahead," Trish said.

"I don't want to be pushy or to make you feel uncomfortable. But I've been wondering, can I talk to you about why you don't want to date? Are you seeing someone already?"

Trish took a sip from her water, stalling while she thought about how to answer. "I'm not seeing anybody. I just don't think it would be a good idea for us to go down that road. Is that going to be a problem for you? If you don't want to hang out, I understand."

June leaned back in her chair, playfully putting a hand under her chin as though she was ready to go into a deep analysis of Trish's motivations. "I didn't say it was a problem. I'm just interested. Why wouldn't we be a good idea together?"

Trish couldn't meet her eye. It felt like June was making fun of her. If it were anyone else she would be thinking about getting up and walking off. She wished she didn't like June the way she did, that she didn't care so much about her opinion. "Well, for one thing, it would be inappropriate. I've met you through work. You didn't even graduate that long ago. What if people saw us together and thought you were a student, and got the wrong idea?"

June frowned. "I don't think it would be inappropriate. We would just explain to people that I've graduated, wouldn't we?"

"Look, I just got here. It might not seem like much to you, but I don't want to take that kind of risk."

"Okay, it's just that I don't really think it's a risk. And I wouldn't tell Ms. Rose we were dating if that's what you wanted," June said.

Trish didn't laugh. That was exactly the sort of thing she was worried about. It was not funny to her that people like Ms. Rose might get the wrong impression.

June shrugged. "If I were still a student I'd understand, but I don't get it. Why am I getting the feeling that's not the real reason?"

"Well, there's also the age difference," Trish said.

"Why, how old are you? I don't know how old you think I am, but I'm twenty-six."

"I'm thirty-five. That's a nine-year gap. I think we're probably at very different stages in our lives."

"I don't think nine years is so bad. Who cares about an age gap unless someone's way too young?" June leaned back and crossed her arms, looking at Trish with her head tilted. "Maybe it's just that you don't like me that way, and it's okay to say that. I'd prefer to just know. I like honesty."

"What I think about you is not really the issue," Trish said tightly.

"How can it not be? I know you're not straight, you mentioned your ex. Or, is it going to be that you're just not ready for a relationship yet?"

Trish barely managed stop herself from snapping. "I've only been single for six months. So yes, it is a little bit too soon for me, but as I've said I have other reasons."

"Hey, I'm really sorry. I didn't know that it was so new." June put her hand on Trish's thigh, just for a moment.

"That's okay."

"Well, I really am sorry I said that. It's just that I'm not asking for a serious relationship right this second. I thought we could just hang out and see what happens."

Trish leaned forward, lowering her voice. June did not seem to care who heard their conversation, but she did. "June, I'm serious about this. I just can't, I'm sorry. I would very much like to be friends with you. I like spending time with you. If my not wanting to date you is going to be an issue, then you're free to let me know."

June waited for a long time before answering, searching her face. "So, you don't ever want to have sex with me?"

Trish coughed, practically choking on air. "Wow. You really don't like to beat around the bush, do you?"

June smirked. "I'm sorry, I'm just making fun of myself at this point. I know I can be a little on the direct side, so thanks for being willing to talk it through with me. I really hope I haven't offended you."

"It's no problem," Trish said. June didn't seem hurt. June's self-confidence gave her a thick skin, one that Trish envied. "I'm glad we had this conversation."

"Me too," June said. She held out her water glass and clinked it against Trish's, sealing the deal.

* * *

Two days later, June came into the library and pushed a book into the returns slot, which was at the counter that Trish was standing behind.

"Hey, how have you been?" June asked, nodding toward her.

Again, this morning Trish had taken care with her appearance. She'd put in contact lenses, and she'd worn a black sweater with a scooped neckline. June's eyes remained trained on her face; they didn't drop down to check her out.

"Good, good. And you?"

Trish took a shaky breath. Since their conversation at the bakery, she'd been nervously waiting to see June again. Though June had seemed fine with everything, Trish worried that if she had time to think about it she might change her mind. They had only known one another a short while, but Trish didn't want to lose her friendship.

"Excellent, thanks. I had last night off, and guess what, I got to watch a whole movie."

"A whole movie? A luxury for you, huh?"

"Heaven," June said, closing her eyes.

"Was it any good?"

"I have no idea, I fell asleep."

Trish laughed. "It's starting to get pretty cold, huh?"

"It is. And it was still dark when I got up this morning. Days are getting shorter for sure."

Trish shifted from foot to foot, cringing at the fact that she'd just resorted to making small talk about the weather. June looked at her watch, then smiled broadly at Trish.

"Anyway, no rest for the wicked. I'll see you later."

June walked away and Trish went over the interaction. June was being polite and friendly toward her, but the warmth and flirtatiousness was missing.

Trish was mortified to admit to herself how very much she missed it.

That night, Trish was draining hot water from a pot of pasta when a knock sounded on the door.

"Come in!" she yelled, transferring the steaming pasta into two bowls.

"Hey, what's for dinner?" Leigh asked, dropping her handbag on the floor with a thud. She kicked off her heels and ran her hands through her hair.

"Hi to you too."

Trish carried the bowls over to the table. She'd laid out extra chili, parmesan, and olive oil. Picking up the oil bottle, she drizzled it over her meal, ignoring the way Leigh was staring at her own dish.

Leigh finally pulled out her chair and sat down. "Trish, are you serving me just plain pasta? What did I ever do to you?"

"Don't be rude. It's pasta al olio."

Leigh shook her head, twirling fettucine around her fork. "Whatever you say. How was your day?"

"Okay, I guess."

"What's the latest with June, have you seen her?"

"I've seen her, sure."

"Hey, this is actually pretty good. And?"

"And, we've agreed it's just friends and friends only. She seems cool with it."

"I don't know why you won't just go for it. She's gorgeous and single, and you have nothing to lose," Leigh said.

"She's not right for me. She's a nice person but she's not girlfriend material, I can tell."

Leigh sighed heavily. "This is your whole problem, you're always like ten steps ahead of whatever's happening. You don't have to marry her, you know. You could just have a bit of fun. She's offering you the chance to just see what happens, with no strings attached."

"That's not me. I'm not going to get involved in something like that, it's too messy. And in any case, she's just not my type. She's not serious about anything, always joking around. She works at a bar. Spending all her time writing a book that'll probably never make a cent. I want to be with someone who has it together way more than she does."

"That's so judgmental." Leigh narrowed her eyes. "You sound exactly like Mom and Dad. You even sound like Katrina. Sorry, but it's true."

Trish picked up their plates from the table and walked them over to the sink, mainly so that she could turn her back on Leigh. Her sister was right, it was an unfair thing to say. There was nothing wrong with working in a bar, and if she heard someone else say that she would be disgusted with them. In fact, she'd often argued with Katrina for looking down on people who had less money than they did. At least June was chasing a dream, doing something that Trish would never have the courage to pursue herself.

"I know it wasn't right. I'm just so sick of always talking about this stuff with you. It feels like all you want to talk about," Trish said.

"Trish, are you scared?"

Trish turned to look at Leigh, forcing herself to meet her eye, leaning against the sink and folding her arms. Leigh had always been able to see right through her, and she was impossible to lie to. Back when Trish was in high school, it was Leigh who'd first raised questions about Trish's sexuality. Leigh joked that she'd dragged Trish out of the closet kicking and screaming, and there was an element of truth to it. "What do you mean? What do I have to be frightened of?"

"You're scared of her, of June. I saw how you were the other night. Not wanting to go near her one minute, staying out all on your own for the chance to hang out with her the next."

"I'm a grown woman, I'm not scared of girls," Trish replied.

"I know you. Katrina was too easy for you, too simple. You never talked about it but we both know you were bored the whole time you were with her."

Trish threw up her hands. "Maybe I was. What's that got to do with anything?"

"You got into a rut you couldn't get out of. Katrina couldn't break your heart because you didn't care enough."

Trish did not bother to argue with that point. What she'd experienced when Katrina left sure seemed like heartbreak to her. Her self-esteem had plummeted, and she had looked around to discover that her life as she had always known it was over.

"What does Katrina have to do with June, anyway? I barely know this woman, and weren't you just accusing me of getting ahead of myself? Why would I be worried about being heartbroken over her?"

"You know what I mean. You don't want someone that can really get to you, you want something safe and predictable."

"You don't actually know everything, Leigh. Do you want dessert or not?" Trish grumbled, slamming the door of the dishwasher shut.

"Yes. And I want ice cream," Leigh replied.

* * *

June stared at the computer screen, jogging her leg up and down and rubbing her eyes. She'd worked an extra shift at the bar on Wednesday night. Because she couldn't afford to take the day off, she dragged herself into the library and was now running on coffee fumes.

She shouldn't have bothered, because she was wasting her time. Anne had sent her a list of suggested articles to look at. It rubbed her the wrong way, because she thought she already had all the sources she needed and felt too exhausted to think about adding more. There were a couple of journal articles that she couldn't locate which only added to her frustration.

A hand came down gently on her arm. "Is everything okay? You look like you're having a rough morning."

It was Trish. June wanted to be at peace with their friendship and most of the time she fooled herself that she was. She had always thought it was pathetic to chase after something that you couldn't have. For the past couple of weeks, she had worked hard to detach herself, knowing that if she acted like she didn't want Trish her mind would eventually follow.

It was unfair to take out her annoyance on Trish. June tried to pull herself together.

"Hey," June said.

Trish grabbed a chair from the opposite desk and sat down next to her. "Can I help you with something?"

June held a couple of fingers to her temple. "I'm fine. It's all good, you don't have to sit with me."

"What is it?"

"Nothing important, I'm just feeling dramatic today. Anne asked me to check out these articles and I can't find them. I have no idea where she even got the ideas, or if maybe she's thinking of something that doesn't exist."

"Can you ask her?"

"I might have to. I was just trying to avoid looking incompetent in case they really are easy to find and this is my fault. I don't have to find them, it's just a suggestion, but the thing is I know she's always right. If she thinks they'll be useful then they will be."

"Show me what she said," Trish said.

June angled her laptop toward Trish and opened the tab that displayed her email. Trish scanned it, then opened a search database, a different system than the one June had been using. She typed in terms, refined them, and within seconds she located the articles that June was looking for. June watched Trish's long fingers roam over the keyboard so elegantly that she could be playing a piano.

"You're good at this game," June said. Just like that, her mood had been turned inside out until she felt calm. Trish lit June up inside.

"I should hope so, it's my job. If you ever need any help, you can always ask me. I'm happy to…whatever you need," Trish said.

June wondered if Trish was aware of the way that her eyes flicked between June's own eyes and her mouth. That train of thought ground to a halt completely when Trish put her hand on June's leg, lightly squeezing and sliding it up the length of her thigh. June jumped at the warm touch that she felt through her jeans.

It took everything June had to not push a hand through Trish's hair. She had started wearing it down now and then, and

June had the urge to touch it all the time. Instead, she put her hand on top of Trish's, gently keeping her where she was.

Trish accepted her touch, her hand unmoving. June watched the rapid rise and fall of her chest, then met her eye again. At times, Trish looked away when it was like this, shifting her gaze elsewhere when she became conscious of how long they'd been staring at one another. Now she stared back, and June had the sense that Trish was daring her to do more.

There were students all around but the desk obscured what was going on between them. Trish's fingers rubbed her thigh and June breathed in, moving subtly closer.

June had always thought of herself as someone whose blood ran a little cool. It wasn't that she didn't enjoy being with women, but to a certain extent she could take it or leave it. It wasn't unusual for her to go for a while without sex or companionship, and that never bothered her. With Trish, though, closeness became a greedy desperate thing, something she couldn't get enough of.

Why was Trish doing this, when she'd said she didn't want it? It could only mean that she'd changed her mind. Hope made June want to be reckless, to kiss Trish here where anyone might see. Instead she remained still, save for her thumb caressing the back of Trish's hand.

Suddenly Trish moved away from her, wheeling back the chair that she was sitting on and returning it. There was nothing in her behavior that showed what had just happened between them, but June was sure that Trish must be masking the same feelings she was having.

"Thanks for your help," June said. When Trish looked back at her, it was with a strange blankness that June didn't know how to interpret.

"You're welcome. Hope those articles are of some help to you, anyway."

"Me too." June put her hands behind her head, trying to slow her breathing as Trish walked away.

Trish was conspicuously absent for the rest of the morning.

CHAPTER SEVEN

"Good morning," June said, grinning at Trish as she passed the front desk.

Trish waved and smiled back at her, relieved to see June acting like everything was fine. All night, Trish had worried about the day before, and what had happened between them. It pulled her close to the surface of sleep, and she'd woken up this morning feeling like sand had been rubbed in her eyes.

Trish shouldn't have touched June like that, especially so soon after they'd had a conversation about just being friends. She was painfully aware that she was sending mixed signals, and she fully expected that once June had time to think about it, she would be mad. In fact, she was so convinced about it that she had been rehearsing her apology. Trish wanted to say sorry before June got too busy, to get it out of the way quickly and clear the air.

Trish looked around and checked that nobody would notice her absence, then went in search of June. Fortunately, there were no students nearby, and the cubicle June had chosen to work in was relatively private.

Trish knocked on the side of it to draw June's attention. "Hey, can I talk to you for a sec?"

"Of course, you can. Pull up a chair." June pushed her laptop closed. "You look nervous. Is this about yesterday by any chance?"

Trish twisted one of her rings around a finger, looking down at the desk. "Yes. I'm not sure if I should even bring it up. But I've been thinking about it. I'm sorry if I made things weird."

June gently took Trish's hands and pulled them away from one another, stopping her from fidgeting. Then June took her hands away, folding them in her lap.

"I'm not mad at you, it's okay. I mean, I was a little confused. You were acting like you…well, you were acting one way and then you were just gone. I feel like you're changing your mind a lot. Talk to me. Help me to know what to think."

Trish took a deep breath. "This is kind of hard for me to admit, but I don't have many friends. I know we just met, but I think we were kind of becoming friends. Can that still happen, do you think?"

"Of course. We don't know each other well, but I like hanging out with you. I'm not going to want to stop just because you touched my leg. I was there too."

"I just don't want you to think I'm playing games or trying to…I don't know…"

"Lead me on?" June said, softening her words with a smile. "I'm not going to pretend it didn't cross my mind."

"Yeah, that."

"Well, what was it about then?"

Trish ran her fingers through her hair. This was much harder than she'd thought it would be, even though June was being kind to her. She wondered why she hadn't just let the whole thing go. Trish hated to think that she might be putting herself in this mortifying situation if she didn't need to.

"I don't even know. Like I said I don't have a lot of friends, and I especially don't have a lot of friends who are, you know, *like me*, so maybe I just don't know how to act?"

"Like you how, exactly? Into books? Lovers of literature?" June said, smirking.

"You know what I mean. Gay."

June cupped a hand around her mouth. "*Gay*. How very scandalous."

Trish covered her face with her hand. "Stop it, this is really hard for me."

"Trish, there's no rule book for how to behave. We're just feeling our way along like any two people who have just met one another, and that's okay. But while we're being super frank, can I ask you something?"

Trish nodded, hands fidgeting again. She wondered where exactly this might be leading.

"Maybe I'm starting to understand why the whole romantic friendship idea was appealing to you. I've been thinking about that since yesterday. You don't want a relationship but there's something about the intimacy of it that appeals to you. It's safe, it doesn't get all complicated by sex. Am I getting warm?"

It was embarrassing to admit it, but June wasn't wrong. That kind of arrangement would be all reward and no risk. A friendship like that would mean that she could feel June's admiration of her, she could even have some physical contact with her, but she didn't have to jump into a relationship that she wasn't ready for.

"I hadn't really put a name to it like that, even when we were talking about it before, but you're probably right. Does that make me an awful person?" Trish asked.

June shrugged. "I'm not here to judge you. It kind of makes sense now that I think about it. It's like when I used to have crushes on straight friends at school. We'd be close, but I never expected anything to happen. Maybe that was just a modern version of a romantic friendship."

"Well, obviously now that we've had this conversation I promise I won't do anything like that again. I'll be more appropriate, I swear."

"What if that's not what I want?"

June's eyes didn't leave hers, and Trish's pulse hammered. To say the least, this was not what she'd expected.

"What are you saying?" Trish asked.

"Why don't we just try it? A romantic friendship? What have we got to lose?"

"What are you talking about?"

"I want to try it. I've been so critical of the idea, but you were right when you said there are all different kinds of relationships. What if we just try to make it our own thing? We agree that we just stay friends, but we can be physical with one another if that's what we want. I'm not talking about sex. But if we feel like hugging, holding hands, whatever, we agree that's okay?"

"What do you get out of it, though? It sounds like I get to have what I want, but what do you get?"

Wouldn't it be terribly selfish to take what June was offering, when she had made it clear that she wanted more? Still, the idea was so tempting, Trish couldn't imagine rejecting it. She wanted to be held by June, to be near her and to be touched by her. And June was forthright; if she said this was what she wanted then shouldn't Trish take her at her word?

"Maybe the same things you're getting. A close friendship. As a bonus, I get to be with you. I can tell you if I think you look especially pretty or if I like what you're wearing. Things I'd hold back from if I had to be concerned with being appropriate, whatever that means. Tell me what you think."

"I think if we're going to do that we have to negotiate an agreement," Trish said.

"That sounds like a good idea. Work out the boundaries so they don't get blurred. Here," June said, opening a new document on her laptop. "I'll even type it up so it's official."

Trish stared at the laptop screen. This was one of the strangest conversations she'd ever had.

"Can I stipulate that we keep this to ourselves? I'm not sure other people would understand."

There was a reason Trish had suggested this condition first. Not only was the idea of anyone else knowing embarrassing, she couldn't imagine how she'd ever explain it to a third party.

June agreed, typing it in as the first bullet point. "What are the physical boundaries for you?" June asked, glancing at Trish's lips.

"Well, I don't think we should be kissing. Not on the lips, anyway."

"Chaste kissing only. I'm putting in that touching over the clothes is fine, and if someone's getting too close we need to have a safe word."

Trish giggled. "A safe word? This is weird. Coffee."

"So weird you know exactly what to pick, huh? Coffee it is. Coffee means back off. Is there anything I'm not allowed to say to you?"

"Like what?"

"I don't know, say I want to use a term of endearment. Call you honey or baby."

"I didn't realize you were the pet name type."

"Well now you know, sugar tits," June replied.

Trish laughed. "Okay, you can call me whatever you want."

"What if I wanted to write about this or talk about it in connection with my book? It's an interesting personal angle."

"You can do that as long as you leave my name out of it, I guess."

"Of course. I guess that's it, really. I can't think of what else we'd need to put in there. We can add to it if we think of anything later."

"I think we should put down that either of us can terminate the agreement at any time," Trish said.

"Oh, that's a good one. With no explanation necessary. If either of us feels uncomfortable, we can pull the pin." June added the last point to the list. "I'll print this out when I get home and give you a copy."

"You don't have to do that, I'll remember everything."

It was so bizarre that she'd recall every word of this exchange. That didn't mean that she wasn't thrilled by it. She wouldn't have to pretend anymore, and the structure they'd just developed made it safe for both of them.

"I'm giving you one anyway, otherwise it's not official. Okay, now shake on it?"

They shook hands firmly, nodding at each other.

"Thank you, June. I'm going to let you get back to work," Trish said.

"Okay. Do you want to meet for coffee tomorrow morning, before you start work? At the coffee cart near the arts building?"

"Sure. I'd like that."

"All right. I'll see you then."

Trish walked away, unable to believe what she'd just signed up for.

The next morning, they met half an hour before Trish's shift began.

"Good morning," Trish said. Though she felt so much better since they'd talked, she was still nervous about how this was going to work out. All night she thought about the agreement, switching back and forth between excitement and the conviction they were doing something crazy and stupid.

"Hi," June said, peeling off her gloves and shaking Trish's hand. June held her hand for a long time, then ran her fingers up Trish's arm.

Trish brushed hair back from her face. If a slightly extended handshake could make her feel like this, she wasn't sure how she was going to cope if things got more intimate. Not that she was complaining.

They walked toward the concrete steps of the arts building. It had been drizzling all morning, and June put her coat down on the damp steps for them to sit on. They settled near to one another on it as students walked up and down the steps around them. It occurred to Trish that June might have chosen this spot because it was away from the library, so it afforded them some privacy.

June dropped her gloves on the step, took a piece of folded paper from her pocket, and handed it to Trish. She didn't need to look at it to know that it was a copy of their contract. Trish slipped it into her handbag without unfolding it.

"Um, thank you. How long have you had the bike?" Trish asked, relieved to find a subject to break the ice.

"A couple of years now. It's the only bike I've had since I got my license. I bought her off a friend's brother. You ever been on one?"

"Never."

"Oh, you're missing out. I'll take you out one day. We could go for a ride outside the city, out to the mountains or somewhere."

"That sounds nice. I'd like to do that."

"So, have you just got the one sister?" June asked.

From that point onward, it was easy. By the time they had finished their drinks, Trish knew about June's two younger brothers and her mother, knew that her parents were divorced and that her father lived overseas. She knew that June had a roommate, a guy that she was very close to.

June asked a lot of questions in return. She was particularly interested in Trish's relationship with Leigh. "I've always wanted a sister," she said.

"You can meet her sometime if you like. She loves meeting people, she's a social butterfly. She's the life of the party, not like me at all."

"I'd love to meet her," June said. "Why do you say that, though? I think you're fun."

Trish pulled a face. "That's not really my reputation."

"Sometimes reputations don't mean much. You're fun to hang out with. I don't just like you for your looks." June elbowed her lightly in the ribs.

"Oh, that's a relief," Trish replied. "And what about you, what's your reputation?"

"I don't know. I think people are surprised I'm a writer, because I'm too outgoing. If I had to sum it up, I'm the class clown."

"See, reputations really are stupid then, because I don't think you're a clown."

"Thank you," June said quietly. She reached out and ran her fingertips down Trish's back over her sweater.

She took her hand away and looked at the time on her phone. "I guess I should be getting to work."

June offered her a hand to help Trish stand up. Trish brushed off the back off her skirt, smoothing it down over her legs. June picked up both of their empty coffee cups and walked them over to a nearby trash can in a few long strides.

"This was nice. It's good for me to take time out and relax, instead of going into work right away. I bet I get more work done now I'm not wound so tight," June said.

Together, they walked to the library.

"We should do this again," Trish said while June held the door open for her. "Are you coming in tomorrow, we could meet then?"

"Tomorrow I'm going to see Anne before class. How about we meet on Friday?"

"See you then," Trish said.

Trish watched June walk away to find a space to work. She liked the security of knowing that they had plans, that she wouldn't have to try and figure out a way to initiate contact again.

Trish hummed while she went to the staff room to deposit her handbag and coat, light and free, feeling like it wasn't a work day at all.

CHAPTER EIGHT

June and Trish quickly established a pattern. Each morning that they were both going to be at the library, they sat on the stairs of the arts building with coffee. A couple of weeks passed in the same way, fall flowing into winter. The season typically inspired melancholy in June, but this year she leapt from bed in the frosty dark mornings.

What had drawn June to Trish was her reserve and her serious nature, and that only made it more gratifying when Trish began to show a different side of herself. Slowly, June was peeling back the layers and beginning to understand more about what kind of person Trish was.

Once, seeing that June was cold, Trish unwound her red tartan scarf and draped the wool around June's shoulders.

"Thank you, but I'm really okay," June said, moving to give the scarf back.

"Please, keep it. You're from sunny Queensland, you need it more than I do."

"I've been here for years! I'm used to the cold by now."

"Oh, I see then. You're afraid that it doesn't go with your uniform."

June laughed. "What uniform are you talking about?"

Trish waved a finger around, pointing toward June's black sweater and gray coat.

"The monochrome thing you have going on. Don't get me wrong, it really works for you," Trish said, suggestively enough that June wanted to lean over and kiss her.

They hadn't indulged in much touching. It wasn't that June didn't want to, but it hadn't felt right so far. At times like these she wanted to hug Trish, or hold her hand, but the place where they met was so public. That didn't bother June at all, but she knew how much it would upset Trish.

It wasn't just that; she also worried about the contract. June knew that instigating it was a weird thing for her to have done, even if it never *felt* strange between them. It would crush her if Trish ever thought that she was being manipulated into anything. The more time June spent around Trish, the more she saw her as someone uniquely kind and intelligent, the kind of woman she'd always imagined herself ending up with.

June settled for sitting close to Trish, for carving out little moments when she could put a hand on her shoulder or help her out of her seat. When she thought she could get away with it, she'd brush her fingers against Trish's hand. June loved watching a certain heat slip into Trish's gaze, and she got off more than she could say on increasing the tension between them.

One day, two weeks after they'd signed their "contract," they were sitting on their stairs. The morning fog had barely lifted, it was so thick that they couldn't see the building across from them.

"I can't get over it. A couple of weeks ago, it was sunny," Trish said.

"It does feel like it set in fast. My mother's gone to Bali. She always goes for a couple of weeks around this time of year. She gets seasonal depression."

"I've never been. Never really travelled actually. Have you?"

"Not to Bali, no. But I travelled around Europe when I finished high school," June said. "Stayed in a lot of crappy hostels. I loved it. I got myself into a few scrapes, drank too much. I met some interesting people, that's for sure."

"That sounds wonderful. My parents offered to send me to Europe after I finished college, but I was too intimidated by the thought of it."

"Why were you intimidated?"

"I don't know, I guess I wanted to just launch into the next part of my life. I went to university right after school and then I was focused on getting a job and building this career. I thought that if I went away it would put me too far behind. And then of course I met Katrina, and she could never get away from work long enough for us to go."

"You never wanted to go, even on your own? If she couldn't?" June asked.

Trish shrugged. "That never really occurred to me, to be honest. And if I had thought of that I don't think Katrina would have liked it."

"Why not? Not even somewhere closer for a couple of weeks, with your sister or something?"

Since she had first heard about Katrina, June had been curious about the woman Trish had shared so much of her life with. Right now, Trish stared off into the fog, avoiding June's eye like the question was painful. June wondered why. She gathered that Trish was struggling with the breakup, but there wasn't a lot of information for her to go on. Trish always avoided the subject and June had never wanted to make her uncomfortable by asking too many questions.

"Katrina was quite possessive in her way," Trish said, as though the idea had just occurred to her.

"How so? Was she the type of girlfriend who wanted to do everything together?"

"Kind of, but that wouldn't be the problem with it. The problem with the idea of me travelling would have been that I would have had experiences that she hadn't. She's a competitive person, very driven. Always needed to be the smartest person in the room. Do you know what I mean?"

"That doesn't sound very fun to be around," June said. She couldn't imagine being with anyone like that, especially not for years of her life.

"I could have stood up for myself more. It was my choice to stay. You know, I think there were people that were relieved when I broke up with her. Not everyone, but some people for sure."

"What did Leigh think of her?"

Trish threw her head back and laughed, the darkness disappearing. "Couldn't stand her. I'm laughing because you should hear some of the names she's started calling her now that she knows it's safe to trash-talk about her. She has the mouth of a sailor."

June pointed a finger for emphasis. "Now see she does sound like fun."

"Actually, I've been meaning to ask you. I'm meeting Andrew and Leigh for lunch on Sunday and I wondered if you'd like to join us. You don't have to if you're busy, but I think you'd like them both. Or if you just want to rest I understand, I know you don't get a lot of time off."

"I'd love to."

June took Trish's hand for an instant and Trish squeezed it. Trish was relieved that she'd said yes, June could tell. June cut her eyes away from Trish's smile, Trish's vulnerability evoking such a pang of tenderness in her that it was overwhelming.

* * *

Trish was the first to arrive at the café, a South American place she'd chosen after coming here for a trial run by herself, the day before. The pale blue and yellow walls were covered in colorful photographs, and they served rich black coffee and cheese arepas she was sure June would love. It was busy and she was happy to see a table with four seats, quickly moving to reserve it. Trish positioned herself with her back to the wall so that she could see the door. Leigh and Andrew weren't far behind her, each of them sporting exaggerated poker faces, their expressions as blank and smooth as she had ever seen them.

When Trish called Leigh to say that she had invited June to lunch, Leigh made a joke about meeting her new girlfriend. Trish gave her sister a stern lecture about how she should conduct herself. There was to be no smirking, no kicking Andrew under the table, and generally no insinuations that Trish and June were anything other than friends. Trish could only imagine Leigh's reaction if she knew about their contract, and Trish had no intention of her ever finding out.

While Leigh rambled about how bad her week at work had been, Trish furtively looked past her to see if June had arrived. When she focused back on Leigh, her sister was looking at her knowingly. Trish chose to ignore it, and when she glanced up again she saw June scanning the room to find them. Trish threw up her hand in a wave and stood up.

"Hey, how are you doing?" June said. After a few long beats, she pulled her gaze away from Trish for long enough to look around at the rest of the table.

"This is my sister, and her boyfriend Andrew," Trish said.

June politely shook each of their hands and said hello, her voice just a little quieter than usual. Trish watched, knowing that Leigh would make up her mind about June within minutes. Leigh was kind, but she was also very quick to make judgments about people, and once she'd formed an opinion about someone it was impossible to change her mind. June slid into the empty chair next to Trish, with Andrew and Leigh sitting across from them.

"So, June, how long have you been at the bar?" Andrew asked once they'd ordered coffee.

"A few years now. I started working there not long after I started studying, it's always been a good way to make money while I focus on other things."

"It's a cool place. So, what part of town do you live in?" Leigh said.

"I'm over in Carlton," June said. "I live there with my friend, Ollie."

"Oh nice, Andrew grew up in Carlton," Leigh said, pointing to him.

"Cool. Where do you guys live now?"

"Elwood. We wanted to be near the beach," Andrew said.

"I love that area. You come to The Dickens a lot though, huh? Let me guess, you must work in the city."

"Sure do, on Collins Street."

Trish poured herself and June glasses of water, happy to just listen. Leigh made eye contact with Trish, nodding slightly to signal that June had met her approval.

"Well, you know me from the bar, so I guess you know what I do, what about you?"

"Andrew's a big brain, he has a doctorate in physics," Leigh said.

"Yep, and now I work at a life insurance firm."

June's fingers brushed against Trish's thigh, and Trish paused as she was lifting her coffee mug to her lips.

"Oh really? That's interesting. What about you, Leigh?" June asked.

"Physiotherapist. I work in private practice."

Trish discreetly slipped her hand under the table and took June's hand, June's thumb sliding sweetly over the back of her hand. It was the first time since they'd made their agreement that they'd been together like this off campus, and she guessed that was why June had initiated the contact.

While they were eating their arepas, their conversations drifted into two separate streams.

"Did you finish that memoir you were telling me about?" June asked.

"I did. Ugh, brutal. I read it so fast because I needed it to be over. It was really well written though."

"Can I borrow it?"

"You want to read brutal, huh?"

"What can I say, you're selling it to me."

Trish wondered if June was paying as little attention to what they were talking about as she was. All her focus was on their joined hands. Trish glanced across the table to make sure that the others weren't noticing anything.

Andrew and Leigh had their heads close together, talking quietly. Leigh nodded emphatically.

"June, we were wondering if you might be free on Friday night?" Andrew asked.

"We're having a little dinner party, and we were wondering if you wanted to join us," Leigh said.

They must have decided that they liked June a lot. Leigh and Andrew regularly held dinner parties for which they cooked complicated meals. They spent weeks beforehand planning menus and bought expensive bouquets of flowers to decorate the house. They supplied carefully matched wines with their dishes. Trish was usually a guest, and had been going more often since she had been single. The rest of the guests were sourced from a rotating roster of Andrew's and Leigh's colleagues and friends. Trish always enjoyed herself, but it was tiring at times to be surrounded by people she didn't know very well. It would be fun to have someone at one of the parties that was *her* friend.

"Thank you so much, but I've got plans next Friday."

"I thought you'd probably be working. She works in a bar, guys, free Friday nights are pretty hard to come by," Trish said.

"No, no," June said. She paused, but then continued, "I've actually got a date."

Leigh threw a concerned look Trish's way.

"They have them all the time, maybe you'll be able to make it to another one," Trish said. June's words had been like a bucket of cold water to her face. She pulled her hand away from June's, picking up her coffee mug with both hands, then looked around for the waiter to refill their coffee, so that she wouldn't have to see Leigh's reaction.

"I'd love that," June replied, withdrawing her hand from where it had been resting, her knuckles against the back of Trish's thigh.

"Great," Trish said.

"Anyway, I should really be going. I've got to get to work. It was really nice to meet you both," June said, rising.

"It was great to meet you too! We need to catch up again soon, I mean it," Leigh said.

"Oh, definitely. See you later."

Leigh and Trish each had their coffees refilled. When Andrew left the table for a moment, Leigh leaned over to her.

"Are you okay? You didn't know she was dating anyone, did you, I could tell by your face."

"No, I didn't know, but why should I mind? She's just a friend. She can date as much as she likes."

Leigh tilted her head and gave Trish another annoyingly compassionate look. "Trish."

"So, who else is coming to the dinner, anyway?"

When she walked out of the café, there was a sense of disconnection for June. With the joy of being with Trish and her family gone, the rest of her day could only be hollow. Over the past couple of weeks, she was finding it more and more difficult to part from Trish's company. Spending time with her only made June want more of it.

It meant a lot to be meeting the people that were important to Trish. A few nights before, when she and Ollie had been having a late-night beer after work, she'd been beaming as she told him about the lunch.

"She wants me to meet her sister...I mean, that's good, right?"

Ollie took a long pull from his beer bottle, eyeballing her the whole time before he wiped his lip. "Mmmm."

"What?"

"You just seem really excited about it. I don't know, maybe too excited under the circumstances. Sorry."

He was right. If he knew what June had proposed to Trish, and their contract, he would flip out. It was wise to not breathe a word to him.

"I've got the best solution in mind for you," Ollie said. "It's actually perfect timing."

"What's perfect timing?" June asked.

"Wouldn't seeing someone else be, like, the best distraction? If you turned out to like her it would be a bonus, but at the least you'll have a fun night out."

"Nah. I'm just not interested in dating right now."

It didn't make sense, but June felt like she'd be cheating on Trish. They were inching toward something special.

"You might be if you met this girl. I hear she's very cute. Max's friend Brie saw your picture in his profile, you know from that night he came to roller derby? Anyhow, she's interested. She asked who you were, and I said I'd talk to you about it."

June picked at the label on her beer bottle. "Look, tell Max thanks, but I don't think it's such a good idea."

It would be so unfair to the unsuspecting woman to use her to get over Trish, and June didn't like playing games. It also wouldn't work. It was impossible that she might meet a woman that she liked as much as she liked Trish. You couldn't force a connection like the one they had.

"I don't think you need to worry if you don't want a relationship right now. From what I hear she's laid-back, a bit of a free spirit, like you. I don't think she's going to get all upset if you don't want it to go anywhere. You could just have some fun, see if you hit it off."

"Maybe."

"Great, I'll text Max and say you're in."

"You know that's not what I said!"

Ollie stared at her with an eyebrow cocked, his finger poised over the screen of his phone.

Maybe agreeing to it made sense. She'd always trusted Ollie's advice. If he was wrong, it would prove to her what she already suspected; that nobody could compare. At least then she'd know.

June threw up her hands. "Okay, okay. You can tell him I'll meet her. But that's it, one dinner."

Messages flew back and forth until her own phone pinged with a message notification. Brie asked if she wanted to go out this weekend, but because June was working she could postpone the date until the following Friday. Now it had been days, and June had not even engaged in some light Internet stalking to find out what she was getting herself into.

Following the lunch with Trish she rectified that, going on to Max's page to find photos of Brie. Brie was blond, and grinning in all the selfies on her page. Though her pose was the same in every picture, her clothes were always wildly different, and she often wore sunglasses or hats. In most of the shots she was flanked by similarly dressed friends, in groups of five or six.

June noted that Brie looked at least a couple of years younger. That might be a problem, because June had decided that she liked the fact that Trish was older than her. It was the sense that Trish had life experience, and June loved the subtle changes that age had brought to her face. Of course, she had no idea what Trish looked like when she was younger, but it was hard to imagine that she hadn't improved with age.

By the time Friday night rolled around, June had talked herself in and out of cancelling the date a thousand times. The most vulnerable moments were after coffee dates with Trish, when she would decide that she couldn't possibly be compatible with anyone else in the way that she was with Trish. They had so much fun just talking and hanging out, to the point where she couldn't remember life as being anything other than boring before they met.

Trish never asked her anything about going on the date, and June didn't want to raise the subject herself. Though she had not intended to tell Trish about it in the first place, part of her had hoped that Trish would react. It would be nice to know that Trish had any feelings at all about it, but it seemed that she didn't care enough to bring it up.

In the end, the date went ahead by default. It reached the point where it would be too rude for June to change her mind yet again.

June met Brie outside of a Korean restaurant in Fitzroy, a trendy suburb just north of the city center. June knew from the messages they'd exchanged that Brie lived nearby in Collingwood.

"Hey there," Brie said, shaking her hand and smiling. She wore high-waisted jeans and a leopard print coat. She tossed her hair, then pinned June with a look.

"Hi. Nice to meet you. Should we get a table?" June asked.

"Sure thing," Brie said, moving to walk inside. As she turned, June saw her profile, and it struck her that there were physical similarities to Trish. Brie was fair-haired, too, and her figure was not that different. With her heart sinking, June knew that it was going to be even harder now to not compare the two of them.

A hostess showed them to their table. The restaurant was sparsely outfitted and would have seemed cold, if not for the candles placed on the tables. Brie picked up the menu and scanned it while June spoke.

"So, how long have you known Max?" June asked.

"A while. We met through friends. It's so nice to see him with a nice boy like Ollie."

"Ollie's great. They're both great," June said.

"They sure are. So, should we order some stuff to share?"

"Sounds good."

"I'll take care of it, I have a knack for ordering the perfect amount," Brie said, making a circle of her index finger and thumb.

When she was ordering, Brie confidently listed dishes, occasionally stopping to ask about ingredients. The hostess left, and Brie leaned toward June, staring at her.

"So, what do you do for a living?" June said, shifting in her chair.

"I'm a graphic designer. I'm freelancing right now," Brie said.

"That's really cool."

"And you?"

"I write, teach a class at Holt. And I work at a bar in the city."

"Which bar?" She leaned further across the table, and June unconsciously leaned back.

"The Dickens."

"Cool," Brie said disinterestedly.

Their drinks arrived, and June quickly reached for her glass of wine. "So, tell me about being a graphic designer? That sounds really interesting."

"Oh okay, we can talk shop," Brie said, rolling her eyes.

"We don't have to if you don't…"

"No, it's just you know how it is when you have a cool job, and everyone wants to talk about it? Although you're right I guess, it is pretty interesting."

"Right," June said. Their food arrived. The portion sizes were so small she was going to leave hungry. She might grab a slice of pizza on the way home.

June listened while Brie talked about her work and then about her ex-girlfriend, politely making encouraging noises when there were pauses in the conversation.

"…And I'm just not that type of a person, like I told her I'm an artist, I need a certain amount of freedom to be able to express myself, no matter what situation I'm in. You know what I mean? You must, if you're a writer."

"Sure," June said, breaking away from eye contact. The rest of the meal crawled by, with June giving up on trying to have a two-way conversation. Brie's favorite subject was herself. When they were done, Brie offered to cover the check, but June insisted on paying her share.

They stood at the front of the restaurant, June shoving her hands in her pockets and looking anywhere but at Brie.

"I've got plans with some friends at One Two Three down the street, you know, the bar on Brunswick Street? Would you like to come?"

"I'm sorry, I've got to be getting home. I need an early night, I've got a lot of work to do tomorrow," June said.

"Oh, come on, you could come for one drink. Max said you were fun."

"I'm sorry, I really can't," June said, smiling stiffly.

"Okay. Well, I'll see you again soon, then."

June stalled, unsure of whether to say anything to make it clear she didn't intend to see Brie for a second date. She could only imagine the grief that Ollie and Max were going to give her for not being open to Brie at all. They would say that she was too biased because of Trish, and they would probably be right.

"Oh, um. Depends on my work schedule and everything, it can be pretty crazy so…" June said.

"No problem, of course. Be in touch?"

"Sure," June said. Brie leaned in and kissed her cheek, the lips soft but dry against her skin.

* * *

All week, Trish wondered about June's date, but she never mentioned it again while they were hanging out. It hurt that June might never have said anything if Leigh's question had not forced the fact out into the open. Trish had been seeing June most days for weeks now, and she thought that they were becoming close friends. Shouldn't dating be something they would share with one another? How many girls was June seeing, anyway?

Trish needed to ask her about it. She wanted to know how long June had been dating someone, and she wanted to gauge how serious it was. The idea of June having a girlfriend was upsetting, if only because it would mean that she would have less time to spend with Trish. Time was in short supply as it was. How long would it be before June might stop meeting her for coffee? It had become important to her, more than she would care to admit.

On the Monday morning following the weekend of June's date, they sat in one of the campus cafés that was based in the sciences building. They'd had to give up on their favorite spot because of the rain that now beat steadily on the roof.

Trish rehearsed the casual way she was going to ask about the date so often, that the words sounded strange as they left her mouth.

"How was your date on Friday?" she asked.

"Good, good," June said, not meeting her eye.

That could mean anything. Maybe June couldn't look at her because she'd spent the whole weekend in bed with her mystery woman.

"So, it went well? Did it?"

June's eyes darted toward her and away. "Actually, no. Not really. I don't think I want to see her again."

"That's a shame," Trish said. "Who was she?"

"Just someone I met through my housemate's boyfriend. She was nice and everything, I just didn't feel like we had too much to talk about."

"You didn't feel like you clicked with her?"

"That's it exactly."

They were quiet, each of them sipping their coffee. When Trish glanced at June's profile, she was lifting the coffee to her mouth, her brow furrowed in concentration. Trish wondered if she was still thinking about the date. Had June slept with this woman? If she was so ambivalent about her, why? Trish wanted reassurance that June wouldn't see her again, but she had no right to ask.

"What about you, did you have a nice weekend?" June asked, finally.

"I did, thanks, it was very relaxing. Did you get up to anything else?"

"I went to roller derby training on Saturday. It's been pretty intense because it's coming up to the finals. We're playing next weekend."

"Tell me again, what exactly is it? All I seem to have absorbed is that you skate," Trish said, laughing.

"It's the best game. I got into it because Ollie's a referee. I went to watch and knew I needed to get in on it. Basically the whole thing is you're trying to score points going around the track the fastest, but there's lots of bashing into each other," June said, smacking her hands together.

"You look quite happy about that?"

"It's an intense sport. See you have two teams and when a team is in play, their jammer is going around here..." she said, using a finger to draw the shape of the track on the table between them. "Trying to get as many points as possible. If you're on the other team, your job is to try and block them from passing you."

"Sounds like fun."

"It's fun to play, it's fun to watch…you know, if you're not doing anything on Saturday night you should come along. Bring your sister and Andrew too, if you like?"

"I'd love to."

June winked at her. "You're in for a treat."

CHAPTER NINE

On Saturday night, Trish sat in the stands of the high school gymnasium, pulse drumming with the anticipation of seeing June play. All around her people ate hot dogs or french fries, children shouting at one another on the steps of the grandstand.

Commentators were set up at a table on the far end of the track, holding microphones and controlling the pumping music.

"Now everyone, get ready for an epic battle between the Melbourne City Rollers and the Hawthorne Harlots!"

It was thrilling to watch as the players took to the track, skating with their arms raised or spinning around as they entered. Trish admired the women's strong bodies, and the refreshing range of shapes and sizes that were represented. The players sped around the track in their skates and helmets, a Bikini Kill song blasting as the commentator introduced them. They wore their colors with hot pants, tights, shorts, and in some cases even fishnet stockings.

"This game will determine who makes it to the semifinals, so let's all make some noise!"

June was wearing tights with shorts over the top of them, and a tank top that revealed more of her arms than Trish had seen before. Her shoulders and biceps were lean and toned. The tank top was tight enough that Trish could also see the roundness of her curves. Trish's mouth went dry as June found her in the crowd and grinned up at her, giving a salute.

The women were all standing in their skates, frozen in place until the buzzer went off. Then they were in motion, and Trish followed June in the pack. As June had explained, there was a fierce physicality to the game, and Trish winced when one of the women tumbled to the ground. Her teammates helped her up again. Trish couldn't take her eyes from June as she weaved around the track, blocking her opponents, skating fast with her chin jutting out.

Leigh and Andrew already had plans for the night, so Trish braved coming here on her own. The idea of going to an event like this alone was terrifying, but she wanted to push herself. Before the game started she had met June at the front of the gym.

June had enveloped her in a hug when she said hello and Trish leaned into it. June kissed her cheek, the soft lips brushing against her skin, and it was all Trish could do to not make a sound or turn her head to press their lips together.

"Thanks so much for coming. Always good to have another cheerleader for the team," June said, releasing her slowly.

"I wouldn't miss it. I'm looking forward to finally seeing what this is all about."

"So, Ollie and I are going to have the team and any friends they want to bring over for drinks after the game. Would you like to come?"

"Of course."

Remembering the way June smiled, Trish worked to pull her focus back to the game in front of her. Although June thoroughly explained the rules, Trish couldn't follow everything that was happening. It was easy to pick out the jammers, because they wore a big star on their helmets. The crowd roared when a jammer was finished rolling around the track. Trish often had trouble figuring out which team was which, though she understood that June was in the Melbourne City Rollers. She watched the numbers change on the scoreboard and let it wash over her, enjoying herself despite the confusion. Trish cheered along with the crowd, raising cold beer and salty fries to her lips.

It didn't matter at all that she was alone, because everybody was too engrossed in the game to notice her. Nobody could know how she felt as she watched June roll around the track, looking so in command of her body. She cringed when June was knocked over as she attempted to block the jammer from the other team, three women becoming tangled in a blur of limbs. June got up again quickly, looking even more determined.

It was nail-bitingly close, and the crowd was in a frenzy by the time the clock had two minutes to go. The jammer for the Rollers was poised, ready to go as soon as the buzzer went off.

"This could go either way folks…the Harlots are ten points up," the commentator said.

The jammer flowed around the track, speeding past the Harlots.

"That's fifteen points for the Melbourne City Rollers, the Rollers claim victory!"

The room erupted into cheers. Spectators moved forward to stand around in a circle while the players rolled around and touched their hands, Veruca Salt blaring from the speakers. Swept along with the crowd, Trish moved to join them. June slapped her hand as she passed, treating Trish to a smile that was just for her.

They'd agreed to meet outside the front of the auditorium and Trish waited. Tonight, she would meet all of June's friends, and she was sure they would find her terribly boring. She couldn't go. It would mean sitting alone in a corner, or even worse, June might feel obligated to babysit her all night. The people at the party would all be roller derby players, girls that were tough and cool in the way that Trish herself had never been. She wasn't any good in large groups. This was definitely not her scene.

June strode toward her. Just the sight of her started Trish's heart racing. June's skates were slung over a shoulder by the laces and she was still wearing her clothes from the game. She'd taken off her elbow and knee pads.

"Congratulations. That was so much fun to watch, really. And you were great," Trish said, touching June's shoulder. June was sweating lightly, and her skin was slick under Trish's fingers.

"Thanks. Hey, do you mind holding my skates? I'm getting cold."

Trish took them from her and watched while June rifled through her backpack to find a sweater. Trish spun the wheels of the skate against her hand. She hated the thought of just leaving, of missing her chance to spend more time with June.

"Ollie's going to be here any minute. He's just packing some stuff up. I can't wait for you to meet him. Just…you know how we said we were going to keep that thing secret? That goes double for Ollie."

"Of course."

"Here he comes."

A short, good-looking guy with red hair and a neatly trimmed beard was walking toward them. He'd added an eccentric twist to his referee uniform with a pair of knee-high rainbow socks.

"Hey. Ollie, this is Trish; Trish, this is Ollie," June said.

"Nice to meet you, Trish."

Trish caught the way he looked her up and down, and she wondered if it was in her head or if he really had taken an instant dislike to her.

"Car's that way," he said, pointing across the parking lot that was next to the gym.

June hung back with Trish while he walked ahead of them.

"Hey, listen, I'm not sure if I can come tonight…"

June stopped and turned toward her, the corners of her mouth downturned under the lights overhead. "Oh."

"I'm sorry," Trish said.

"We can give you a ride somewhere if you want."

"That's okay, I can just catch the train."

"It's dark. I'd really feel better if we dropped you off? I mean, if you have to be someplace else, we can just take you to a station?"

June's shoulders slumped; she was deflated after being so happy just moments ago. Trish didn't want to leave her, and it seemed like June really wanted her to come to the party. Trish told herself to be brave. "You know what, I'll come to your place. The other thing can wait."

June grinned, gesturing toward the car. "You want the front seat?" she asked, holding the door open.

"No, please, you take it."

Trish moved into the backseat, sitting in the middle so that she could lean forward and hear June and Ollie talking.

"So that new jammer is pretty good, huh?" Ollie asked.

"Oh yeah, she is super-fast." June looked over her shoulder at Trish. "That's the one who races around and gets all the points."

Trish nodded, and glanced over at Ollie. His eyes flicked toward her in the rearview mirror, looking at her blankly. Trish was finding him difficult to read, but there was a coldness about him that surprised her. June's description had given Trish the impression that Ollie would be much nicer than he was. Trish wanted him to like her, but more importantly she wanted to like him. So far it was a mystery to her why June and Ollie were so close.

"Is Max coming tonight? I didn't see him at the game," June asked.

"He was out having dinner with some friends, but he'll be over at our place soon. Oh, and I'm sorry to tell you this, but he's bringing a few people. Brie's going to be in the group."

Trish stared out of the window. If she had known that Brie was going to be coming, she would have listened to her instincts and gone home. She wished could have a private moment with June to talk about this, to see if she should make herself scarce. She couldn't imagine talking about it with Ollie here, though.

"I wish he'd asked if he could bring her. It's a little weird," June finally replied.

"I know, I know. But I don't think it's his fault. She caught wind of it and insisted."

"I don't know why she would do that, though? I called her and told her thanks, but that I didn't want it to go anywhere. I don't know what more I can do."

"Maybe she just wants to hang out as friends then. She'll probably be cool about it all," Ollie said.

"Maybe," June said. Trish caught another look from Ollie. She met his eyes and then looked out of the window again. She shouldn't be here.

When they arrived at the apartment, June offered to show her around. There was a strong lemon scent like the place had been scrubbed down, and now it was clean but untidy. There were stacks of books and records everywhere. As they walked down the hallway Trish glanced into the bedrooms to find that both June and Ollie slept on mattresses on the floor. Furniture was scarce, and milk crates and boxes served as tables here and there. Almost every wall was covered with paintings. June explained that most of the pieces had been given to them by artist friends.

As they walked out of sight of Ollie, Trish put a hand on June's waist. There weren't many opportunities for them to do this, and she wasn't about to let it go by. June turned and pulled her into an embrace. Trish's breath quickened as they were pressed against one another.

"I love your glasses, but I like being able to see your eyes. They're really pretty," June said.

"Thank you. You have...you looked good in your playing clothes," Trish replied, catching herself before she said anything more explicit. It really wasn't like her to comment on someone's body.

"Is this okay? Do you need to say coffee?"

"No, it's nice," Trish said. "Thank you for inviting me tonight."

Trish closed her eyes. June's body was soft and hard against her at the same time, and June's hands were on her waist, rubbing small circles over her clothes. She could stay here all night, breathing June in. Trish wondered if June might feel the same way, because it took a long time for her to let Trish go.

They finally returned to the kitchen, Trish trailing uncertainly behind June. Ollie had changed his clothes and was pottering around, wiping down the countertops. The blender was surrounded by liquor bottles.

"I'm just going to have a shower before everyone gets here. That cool?" June asked. Trish nodded toward her, leaning against the kitchen table casually as though she wasn't terrified about being left alone with Ollie.

"Cool," Ollie said, hitting the start button on the blender so that the room filled with the sound of grinding ice.

Ollie kept his back toward her as Trish sat down at the kitchen table. When the blender stopped, Ollie finally looked over at her.

"Can I get you a drink?"

"Yes, please, that would be great."

Ollie mixed her a margarita, expertly dipping the rim of the glass in salt. Trish remembered that he worked in a bar just like June did.

"This is great. Thank you."

Ollie nodded, as though it were a given that his drink-making skills were perfect.

"So, you work at the university library, right?" Ollie asked.

"That's right. Just started not too long ago."

It was quiet, and Trish tried to think of something to say.

"Can I help you with something?" Trish asked.

"You can slice these up if you like."

She was given a cutting board and a pile of lemons and limes to work on. Trish's eyes fell on a novel on the table, a coming-of-age story called *Infinity* by C.M. Bowles. In high school it had made her feel less alone, cutting through her isolation like only the best stories could. A bookmark was tucked into the pages toward the end. Trish wiped juice from her fingers and picked up the well-worn paperback.

"I love this book. Are you reading it or is it June's?"

"That's mine," Ollie said. "You've read it?"

"Oh yes, more times than I can count."

"Really? It's been like my bible since I was about fourteen years old."

"Me too. Well, I read it a couple of years later than that, but I reread it every year at least. It's like coming back to an old friend."

"I know! Have you read her other stuff?" Ollie asked.

"I have every single one. Even that awful short story collection they rushed out when she died."

"Oh, totally agree with you. But one simply must have it. Check this out," Ollie said, pulling up the sleeve of his shirt. Trish ran her fingers over his tattoo, across the Latin phrase "de omnibus disputandum."

"Question everything, right? Now that's next level commitment, I love it."

When June came back, Ollie was leaning on the countertop to talk to Trish, their drink-making forgotten.

"What are you guys talking about?" June said. When Trish held up *Infinity*, June rolled her eyes.

"I don't know how he can keep reading it again and again," June said.

"Blasphemy!" Ollie cried, and Trish nodded eagerly.

"You can't just read it once or twice, it's way too layered. You get something different out of it every time," Trish said.

June smirked at Trish, shaking her head.

When June passed by to make herself a drink, Trish caught the fragrance of June's soap, something deliciously fresh. June had changed into tight black jeans and a soft gray sweater. Trish watched her reaching for bottles and contemplated the flawless shape of her bare feet. Trish had never appreciated a woman's feet before. What was she turning into?

Soon the first guests arrived, and before long the kitchen and its surrounding rooms were full of people and the buzz of conversation. Music played, the speakers in the living room blasting a 1960s girl group singing about boys. Trish shook a lot of hands as June introduced her to friends. Most of the people she met were women from the roller derby league, joined by friends or partners, both male and female. They washed over Trish in a sea of tattoos, piercings, and effortlessly cool clothes.

It all made her feel square and boring, just like she knew that it would.

"This is my friend Trish," June said again and again. There were women who greeted Trish with jealousy, as though trying to figure out if there was more to the story that brought this stranger to them. It wasn't surprising that so many of these women had a crush on June, and Trish wondered how many of them June had already slept with. There had to be a reason they all came across as so possessive. The thought made her clench her teeth.

It soothed her frustration that June stayed by her side, not leaving her alone for a second. June kept grabbing her shoulder or running her fingers down her arm, especially when nobody was watching. It made her feel cared for, and Trish never had the sense that June wanted to be anywhere else. Now and then June would turn toward her and whisper something conspiratorially, a piece of gossip about this person or that.

A group of people entered the room, drawing shouted greetings, and when Trish looked at June, her jaw looked tight. Trish easily clocked Brie, a blond woman whose gaze had started to cling to June as soon as she came in. The gaze slipped across to Trish, running up and down her body in assessment. Brie's expression told her clearly how she had been scored. Brie had decided that whoever Trish was, there was nothing about her that was a threat.

"I should say hello to Max, and Brie," June said. "I'll introduce you to them."

Trish followed June across the room, watching the group and seeing Ollie kiss his boyfriend hello.

"Hey Brie, Max, everyone. Guys, this is my friend Trish," said June.

"Hello," Brie said, taking Trish's hand between the two of hers, glaring nakedly at her as she did it.

"How are you?" Trish said.

Brie didn't answer, looking over Trish's shoulder like she was scanning the room for someone better to talk to.

"Hey, I'm going to go and get a drink," Brie said, stepping close to June and laying a hand on her waist. She shot another dirty look at Trish before she walked away.

Trish glanced at Ollie, who was watching the exchange with an amused expression.

As soon as Brie and her group drifted over to the table where the drinks were set up, June took Trish's arm.

"I'll show you where the bathroom is," June said, leading Trish down the hall. When they were alone she put a hand on Trish's shoulder. Trish moved nearer to her.

"I'm so sorry, Trish, I can see that she's being really rude to you already. This is what I was afraid of when Ollie said she was coming. I would never have invited her here."

"She is being rude, isn't she? The way she looked at me…it's like she's jealous. Like she thinks we're together or something. Is she like that with everyone?"

"I don't know! But she's being weird. It just proves that I was right to keep my distance from her in the first place, I didn't like her whole vibe. I kind of can't believe it, I only went on one date with her. We didn't even kiss or anything."

"You really didn't kiss her?"

"No," June said. "I didn't want to."

June put a hand on Trish's shoulder again and Trish felt the gentle weight of it through her shirt. As someone passed them in the hall, June leaned closer. "I'm going to tell Ollie this as well, but can you please rescue me if it looks like I need it? I don't think Brie's going to leave it at that, I feel like she'll definitely try and talk to me again."

Trish shivered at the feeling of June's breath so close to her ear.

"Of course, I will. You can count on me," Trish said.

June pulled away, her expression lighting up to see Ollie approaching them.

"I came to see if you need reinforcements," he said, grinning.

"I think we do Ollie, I think we do," June said.

Ollie gleefully put his arm around them, drawing them into a huddle. Trish buzzed with the feeling of being included by the two of them.

"So, ladies, what are we going to do about the bunny boiler?" he said in a stage whisper.

"That's just what we're trying to figure out," June said. "I have a feeling she's going to try to talk to me again. I've just asked Trish to help me out if I look like I'm stuck. The goal is to separate me from her if you ever see her trying to pin me down. Just come in and find any way to take me away, say you need something, whatever."

"You got it, I'm in. And next chance I get I'm going to tell Max to not invite her to stuff like this. She can be a strictly Max friend, at least while you're around."

With their agreement in place, the three of them moved back into the kitchen.

"Hey Trish, want to be my apprentice, help me make some more drinks?" Ollie asked.

"I would love to."

"Okeydokey, can you pass me the rum? It's mojito time."

Trish searched through the bottles until she located it. "Isn't it a bit cold for mojitos?"

"It's never too cold for mojitos," he said, pointing a muddler at her. "Can you cut some more limes while I get going on this mint?"

"Of course. And I like the way you think. How long have you and Max been together?"

Trish searched the room to find June, who was mingling with the guests.

"About a year. I hit the jackpot with that boy. So, what do you think we should make after the mojitos?" Ollie said, glancing up.

"I'm not sure…"

"Oh dear. I think we've got a situation. Code Brie," he said. He had his hand covering the blender lid as the motor whirred loudly. "I think you should get in there."

"On it," Trish said, eager to help. There was nothing that she would like more than to interrupt Brie and June. June was leaning away from Brie, who was speaking to June with a raised finger.

Trish moved as fast as she could and slid into place next to June, the urgency making her put a possessive arm around June's shoulder.

"Hey. Sorry to interrupt. June, Ollie and I were hoping you could help us with the drinks. It's getting hard to keep up with the demand."

"Um, can't you, like, deal with it yourself?" Brie said. "We're in the middle of something."

June looked at Brie with widened eyes. Normally Trish would withdraw from a situation like this in favor of minding her own business, but June had asked for her help. Trish couldn't go back to Ollie and tell him that she'd failed at the mission, not when he'd asked her to do this.

"No, we really need her. She's the hostess," Trish said. "She has to do hostess things."

"She can do them later. We're talking," Brie said.

"Excuse me, Brie," June said. "But I really should go."

"Who exactly are you, anyway?" Brie asked Trish. "Are you two seeing one another? You do know she and I just went on a date last week, right?"

Trish tightened her grip around June's shoulder. "Oh, that's okay. I don't mind if she goes on a date now and then, as long as she always comes home to me. We've got that kind of relationship. Don't we, honey?" Trish said.

June quickly caught on to the ruse, putting her arm around Trish's waist. "Yes. I'm very sorry Brie, I should have told you about this."

Brie was looking back and forth between them, not buying it. "You're telling me this is your girlfriend? Why wouldn't Max tell me that you had a girlfriend?"

"I have no idea. I guess because of the whole open relationship thing, but Trish still gets a say in what I do. I mean, that's how we make it work. Anyway, I should go and help," June said. "Sorry."

They walked away holding hands, June's palm brushing softly over her skin.

When they got to Ollie, he nodded at Trish. "Did you just do the fake girlfriend maneuver? If so, I'm totally impressed."

"I did. I didn't know what else to do," Trish said, reluctantly dropping June's hand. It had all seemed like a game, but the embarrassment was starting to sink in now. "I'm sorry, June. I hope I haven't made things even worse, that was all really silly."

"Not at all, it wasn't silly. I don't care what she thinks as long as she leaves me alone. She was being impossible. I'm just worried she didn't really believe it anyway."

The three of them looked over to see that Brie was now speaking with Max. Max was shaking his head, his hands lifted up by his sides. June covered her face.

"Oh shit. He's telling her that we were making it up. This is the worst."

Brie glared at them. Ollie put his hand to his mouth and bit the skin between his thumb and finger, his shoulders shaking.

June hit him on the chest. "This is not funny."

"It is. I love dyke drama, it's the best."

He sobered suddenly when Brie started marching toward them.

"Golly, she's crazy. Why wouldn't you just leave at this point?" Ollie said, as though he were watching a character on a television show.

"What do I do, what do I do?" June said.

"Double down. Kiss her, Trish," Ollie said.

Trish looked back at him and tried to laugh because he must be joking, then she met June's eyes. June was looking back at her, her expression neutral, but she was fidgeting and shuffling around.

Trish placed her hands on June's hips.

She leaned forward.

It would only be a peck, a kiss as chaste as could be. It was against the rules, but this situation warranted an exemption, she was sure of it.

Trish's lips touched June's and a gasp passed between their mouths when they made contact. Thanks to the cocktail she'd been drinking, June tasted like salt and citrus. In her wildest imaginings, Trish had not thought June's mouth would feel so right against hers. Trish pulled back and traced her fingers over June's lips, and June's eyes looked into her own, asking her for more. There was no question of not giving it to her. Trish eagerly leaned in once more.

Trish had meant for it to only be for another moment, yet the kiss went on and on. They savored one another's lips, the room dropping away. June's mouth was so warm and inviting, and as soon as Trish's mouth opened, June followed her. June's tongue gently explored hers. Trish put her hand on the back of June's head to keep her close, her hand playing through June's hair. June's soft breasts were pushed up against her chest.

If they were alone, she would be pushing June against the countertop by now. She would be touching her everywhere. Trish never wanted to stop kissing her.

June's hand had dropped to the small of Trish's back, settling there in a way that suggested it wanted to move lower. Trish wished that it would. She had never had a kiss like this.

"Uh, you guys. You can stop now, she's leaving," Ollie said.

They pulled apart in slow motion and stared at one another, each of them breathing fast.

"Drink anyone?" Ollie asked, holding out the jug.

CHAPTER TEN

Memories from the night before flooded back to June as she stirred. What a strange evening. Brie's arrival at the party had thrown her, and having both her and Trish in the same room was more than a little weird.

It was strange to have Trish in her house in the first place, to see her at ease in the kitchen talking a mile a minute with Ollie. By the end of the night, Trish and Ollie had been acting like old friends, which June loved. Trish fit neatly into her life; she belonged in it.

Trish had been different last night, looser and more relaxed. For the first time Trish had initiated things with her, touching her as they walked around the house. Trish's slight tipsiness allowed her to fix her gaze on June a little more openly than she normally would. Trish's stare dropped to her chest, and June turned around more than once to see Trish quickly raise her gaze back to her face.

There had been more guests than she and Ollie were expecting. Word had gotten around, and a lot of extra people tagged along. Their few rooms had been stuffed full of friends and strangers until the early hours of the morning. Eventually both Ollie and June had slipped off quietly to their bedrooms, leaving the house to their guests in the hope that they would all be gone by morning. June was sure the house was a mess, but she hoped there wasn't any serious damage.

The memory that she was avoiding surfaced. The intensity of that kiss had shocked her, and shocked her still. There had always been something so sexy about Trish, a quality that peeked out from behind that buttoned-down façade that she presented to the world. Now June had caught a glimpse of it in the way Trish kissed, sighing against June, grabbing her hair. June wanted to see much more of that side of her. She had a feeling that it wouldn't disappoint.

June rubbed her eyes and picked up her phone. There were two missed calls from Trish, and June pressed the button to call her back.

"June?"

When June spoke, her voice left her mouth in a rasp. She had been shouting to make herself heard over the music all night. She cleared her throat. "Hey Trish."

The line was quiet.

Trish left the party half an hour following Brie's dramatic departure. After the kiss, they had acted like nothing had happened between them. They stayed where they were, joking with Ollie about the crazy way that Brie behaved. Max joined them and apologized for bringing Brie over, saying that he hadn't known what her agenda was when he'd agreed to bring her. Ollie poured them all another round of drinks and as soon as Trish finished hers, she excused herself to go and call a cab.

Trish leaned against the wall with a finger in her ear, trying to block out the noise as she gave directions to the driver. Words could not capture how badly June wanted to take the phone from her hand, and tell her that she should stay. It wasn't even that June wanted to kiss her again, although of course she did want that. It was that June wanted to sleep in the same bed as Trish, even if nothing else happened between them. June just wanted to hold Trish in her arms.

"Trish? Is everything okay?" June said.

"I guess I just wanted to make that we're okay, after last night."

June sat up in bed, clutching the phone in her fist. Of course, Trish would think that she was mad at her. They weren't supposed to kiss one another, they'd even written it down. But the night before had been such a strange situation, with Brie backing them into a corner and Ollie egging them on. Maybe the kiss had weakened her even more against Trish, because she couldn't find it within herself to be mad.

"It's okay. I get how it happened. It's not your fault."

"Thank you. I was really worried."

"No, I should be thanking you. You really helped me out of a bad situation," June said, lying back down and settling against the pillows. She couldn't talk any more about the kiss without saying something stupid, so she changed the subject. "How are you doing? I don't feel that great."

"Me neither! I haven't had a hangover like this for a while."

"Bacon and eggs, best cure you'll find. Did you have fun last night?"

"I did! I love Ollie, he's so nice. So was everyone else. Well… aside from Brie."

June laughed, putting her hand on her forehead. "I know. She really was too much, wasn't she?"

"Indeed. But it's okay. I should take your advice and have something to eat. See you tomorrow morning?"

"Same time, same place."

June sighed when they hung up. They had never spoken on the phone before. Talking to Trish had made her feel like she was right here, her voice soft in her ear. June was lying with an elbow thrown over her face when Ollie dragged himself into her room and flopped down on the bed next to her.

"I'm scared to go out there. The place must be a mess," he groaned.

"It'll be okay," June said, listlessly patting his arm.

Ollie turned to the side and pulled her elbow from her face. "So. Trish. Let us talk about Trish."

"Mmmm," June said. It made her feel exposed to think that they had kissed in front of everyone, although June didn't usually care about things like that. It must have been obvious that she was very into Trish. June had been desperate to prolong that kiss, and had not cared enough at the time to try to hide it.

"I thought when I met her that she was going to be…I don't know exactly, but I like her," he said.

"What do you mean? What did you think she was going to be like?" June held her breath to hear what Ollie might say next.

"You know what I mean. I thought she was going to be full of it. But she's real nice, real genuine. And she likes you. Like, really likes you. She couldn't take her eyes off you all night. I really don't understand why you guys haven't gone there."

"She just doesn't want to get into anything with me. That's what she says."

"I think she doesn't know what she's doing. I don't know, there's something about her, like she just doesn't know herself very well, do you see that?"

"Who knows." June was becoming tired of discussing it and even more tired of thinking about it. She was prone to melancholy when she was hungover, and thinking about Trish this much was starting to hurt. Why did she want it so much, when she might never have it?

June poked Ollie in the stomach. "Okay, dude, we need to face the music."

They rolled out of bed in unison.

After she hung up, Trish checked the time. It was past ten and she had no plans for the rest of the day. It was more than a hangover that was making her jittery right now. It was difficult to remember a time that she'd ever been so turned on, and all from just a kiss.

The contact with June's body had been like kindling, setting her alight.

There was an obvious thing that she could do to get some release, but she didn't want to go there. It would make her think only of June. It would bring back the softness of her mouth, and the muscle under her fingers as she'd moved her hands up June's arms, toward her throat and into her hair.

Trish forced herself to get out of bed so she would stop thinking about all of that, and changed into leggings, trainers, and a black hoodie. She jogged down to the nearest dog park and circled it again and again. As her feet pounded on the earth, she ran harder and harder until she was conscious only of the burning sensation in her legs, her chest opening until breathing was easy. Trish needed to use her body like it was a machine, to forget what she really wanted to use it for, how much she wanted June to touch her. She ran for over an hour, sweating out toxins with her thoughts.

When she arrived home, she wondered if she hadn't overdone it. She must be hallucinating.

Katrina sat on her front step. Trish slowed to a walk, ripping her headphones from her ears. Something must have happened. Someone must be sick or dying for Katrina to be here like this without even calling her first.

"Katrina? What's going on?"

Katrina stood up, her arms raised as though she was going to try and hug Trish, but she dropped them when she saw the look on Trish's face.

"Hello. Can we talk?"

Trish put her hands on her hips, still catching her breath. Her face must be beet red, and she was covered in sweat. Katrina had not apologized for the intrusion. Katrina never apologized for anything.

"You couldn't call me first?"

Katrina's eyes widened. For just as Katrina never apologized, Trish never demanded that she do so.

"Is this about the house or something?" Trish asked.

"It's nothing like that. I honestly just want to talk. Please, can I come in?"

Trish walked past her, up the steps to the front door. She was too curious to not have this conversation.

"I'd like to clean up if you don't mind. You can come in."

As they moved inside Katrina looked around. "Wow, you've...it looks different."

"Made some changes. Maybe you can make a pot of coffee while you wait," Trish said.

"Of course."

Trish left her in the kitchen. As she stood under the hot needles of water, she thought about the fact that the woman who had lived with her for so many years was a now a guest in the next room. If she knew Katrina at all, her ex would poke around their house for as long as she could hear the shower water running. *Her* house.

Let her look, Trish thought. Let her see how different I like things to be when I get to have a say in anything.

Trish dressed in sweatpants and a shirt, not making any effort. Katrina was always fashionably dressed. Today she was wearing crisp, dark blue designer jeans with a sweater, Italian leather boots, and a very expensive silk scarf. Trish was drying her hair with a towel when she came out to find Katrina in the dining room. There was a pot of coffee and two mugs on the table.

Before Trish sat down, Katrina looked her up and down. Trish had never been as lean as she was now. After the separation, Trish needed to focus on something that made her feel good, so she'd started running. She had gotten quick results.

"You're looking very well, Trish," Katrina said. "How are you?"

"Thanks," Trish said, pouring herself coffee. "I'm a little tired, I was out late last night."

"Oh? What were you doing?"

"I was at a party. What's this all about?"

"I was thinking about you."

"And?" Trish said.

"It doesn't feel right sometimes. That we shared so much of our lives together, and now we're like strangers."

Trish frowned. She had struggled to reconcile that herself, but she always got the impression that Katrina left without looking back. It was heartbreaking that during all their talks, Katrina hadn't expressed a single doubt about them breaking up. She had laid out the argument methodically like she was in front of a courtroom. She explained that they'd grown apart, that Katrina's feelings had changed, and that it was the same for Trish even if she couldn't admit to it. Katrina didn't want a trial separation or to try to salvage the relationship; she just wanted to end it.

"I thought we agreed that we weren't going to be friends. We talked about this. It's gotten easier for me lately, hasn't it gotten easier for you too?"

Katrina was staring down into her mug, uncharacteristically hesitant. "Sometimes. But I still miss you."

Katrina reached for her hand, and Trish let her take it for a few seconds. Then she pulled it away and let it rest back on her mug.

"So, what are you saying, you want to catch up for coffee now and then?"

"I want to start seeing one another again. We can take it slow but…"

"What about your girlfriend?" Trish asked.

"We've broken up."

Trish crossed her arms. Katrina had been dumped, and now she was seeking comfort in the familiar. Trish was someone she assumed would be there whenever Katrina felt like picking her up again.

"Why are you looking at me like that? I broke up with her, I'm not rebounding back to you, if that's what you're thinking!"

"You left me. I've moved on. And so have you. I think you're just feeling lonely. I'm not here just to make you feel better."

"Trish, it's not like that. I miss you. All I can think about is that I made the biggest mistake when I left you. Left us, left this house."

Katrina's voice wavered, tears spilling from her eyes. She had barely cried during the breakup, and was never one to cry during fights. It had always gotten under Trish's skin to see Katrina cry, rare as it was. She quickly moved to get some tissues.

She put the tissues in front of Katrina and sat back down. Trish didn't trust herself to hold her, afraid of the feelings that it might bring up. Even a month ago, this would have felt like a beautiful dream. Recently she had ceased imagining it, and had ceased even wanting it to happen. She'd missed the point where it had ticked over, because somewhere along the way she had finally stopped paying attention to any thoughts about Katrina. Yet Trish could not deny the fact that this was affecting her.

"Are you seeing someone?"

Trish shook her head, cutting her eyes away.

"Has there been anyone else, since me?"

Trish didn't answer. She didn't want Katrina to know that she was the last person that Trish had so much as kissed, but then she corrected herself. Last night Trish had kissed someone else, and it had been the kind of earth-shattering kiss that she had never shared with Katrina.

"Maybe we could just date for a while. I could take you out for dinner and we could just see how it felt?" Katrina said.

"I don't know. I really need to think about all of this. This is so out of the blue for me."

"Of course, you need to think about it. I understand completely. Let's just make a date for next Friday night, and you can let me know if you don't want to come."

It was such a transparent negotiating technique, making Trish agree to something so that it would take more effort to back out. Still, she might as well say yes, if only so that Katrina would leave her alone for now. She needed time to herself to think about everything that had happened, not just today but last night with June as well.

Trish nodded, then got up to clean up their mugs so that she wouldn't have to see the satisfied look on Katrina's face.

That evening, Trish prepared for their regular family dinner. Since their parents' divorce three years earlier, Leigh and Trish took turns hosting the meal. The schedule gave equal time to each parent, and tonight was their dad's turn.

Leigh arrived first, carrying a boxed cake. "Is he here yet?"

"Nope."

"Good. I wanted to ask about your date!" Leigh said, putting the cake down on the kitchen table and rubbing her hands together.

"It wasn't a date. I told you I was just going to watch her play roller derby."

"And was that it?"

"I went to a party at her house, afterward."

The bell rang, and Trish bolted for the door. She didn't know how much longer she could spend around Leigh without spilling everything. Although it was tempting, Trish wasn't ready to deal with her reaction. Leigh would be livid about Katrina showing up on her doorstep like that. It was for the best if she avoided talking about June. She was still trying to work out how she felt, which was hard enough without Leigh pushing her agenda.

"Hey, Dad," Trish said, opening the door wider to let him in.

He shook rain from his umbrella and laid it on the ground, rubbing a hand over his graying hair. A retired high school English teacher, he still looked the part in his V-neck woolen sweater worn over a collared shirt.

"Hello sweetheart," he said, kissing her cheek and passing her a bottle of wine. "Is your sister here yet?"

"Yes, she just got here," Trish said.

Trish had set everything up on the dining table and they sat around, tucking into their steak and vegetables.

"So, Dad, has Trish told you about the hot young thing she's been hanging out with lately?" asked Leigh.

Their father's eyes sparkled while he looked at Trish. He had always been very comfortable about Trish's sexuality, and often asked about her romantic life. Sometimes he was just as incorrigible as Leigh, although their opinions differed. Each of Trish's parents thought that Katrina had hung the moon, and had been devastated when they'd split up.

"And who is the lucky young lady?" he asked.

"We're just friends. There's nothing to talk about," Trish said. Images of June and her sweet-tasting mouth ran through her mind even as she issued the denial.

Leigh shook her head at their father. "Don't bother. But mark my words, they're not going to be just friends for long."

Trish rose to refill their water glasses, hoping they'd get the hint and change the subject.

"I'd love to see you in a new relationship, honey. Look at Leigh, she's settling down. You're going to have to think about it one of these days yourself."

"Why do I have to do that? I haven't even been single for a year. I don't have to be with anyone if I don't meet the right woman. You are two peas in a pod, honestly."

Trish rolled her eyes when Leigh and their father exchanged a knowing look.

"I just wish you'd tried harder with Katrina. She was so perfect. You shouldn't have let her go," he said. He shook his head wistfully, as though the break-up belonged in one of the Shakespearean tragedies he'd spent his life teaching.

Leigh was silent, but she was obviously itching to offer a conflicting point of view. Normally Trish would bite her dad's head off for a comment like that, but it was different after seeing Katrina.

"Why do you think she was perfect, Dad? What exactly was it about her, and us, that makes you think that?"

He put down his knife and fork and took a long draw of water. "Well, it's nice to know you want my opinion about this for once. You two have the same values. Katrina's a hard worker, she's great with money. She knows what's important in life. There was always something so steady about her."

Was it steadiness that made someone a great partner? Did it not matter to him that Trish and Katrina just fundamentally didn't get along? Sometimes she realized that she and Katrina had been better at putting on a show than she had even realized.

"So, to be clear, you would be happy if Katrina and I were to get back together."

"Over the damn moon," he said. "Why, is there a chance that might happen?"

Trish looked at her father and then her sister, each of them sitting frozen with their knives and forks in the air. To frighten the latter, Trish shrugged. "You really never know."

CHAPTER ELEVEN

June woke up from a dream that was full of flaxen hair brushing against her face, and the sensation of a kiss upon her lips. June stretched her arms over her head with it all fresh in her mind, her toes curling. It wasn't the first time she'd dreamed about Trish, but this one had reached a whole new level of vividness.

The first semester at Holt was over, which meant a two-week break from her class, not that a break meant that much to her. It wasn't a vacation because she would still have to write and work at the bar. At least her schedule was slightly less crazy when she didn't have to tutor on top of everything else. Today she didn't have to work at all, and she planned to devote the entire day to writing.

When she arrived, Trish was already waiting for her at the coffee cart. June wasn't sure what things would be like after their kiss. They had worked so hard to get to this point in their friendship and she didn't want to blow it now.

"Hey. Did you enjoy the rest of your weekend?" Trish asked, playing with a piece of hair that had escaped from her bun. June considered reaching out to push it behind her ear. She knew now what it felt like to touch Trish's hair, how soft it felt under her fingers.

Screw it, June decided. There was hardly anyone around. She reached forward and let her hand linger on the side of Trish's face once she'd moved the hair. Trish's breath caught.

"I did, thanks. I was a little tired doing my shift at the bar on Sunday. How about you?"

"Oh…nothing to report, really. My dad and Leigh came over for dinner."

"That sounds nice."

They drank their cups of coffee slowly on the steps, neither of them in a rush to go inside.

"Wow, it's like a ghost town around here," June said when they finally walked into the library together.

"It is. We're on a skeleton staff. Not many students are as dedicated as you are about your writing."

"Or maybe they're just not as dedicated to being around good-looking librarians as I am," June said, raising her eyebrows at Trish. Trish grinned back at her.

"That was very cheesy," Trish said.

"I agree. And you loved it."

June arranged her things on the desk, enjoying the ritual of laying everything down on the table before she uncapped her pen and smoothed out the page of her notebook. There was only a handful of students scattered around the room. The quiet should be helping her to concentrate, but her mind was too occupied today. It was impossible to measure how many minutes she'd wasted in the time since Trish had started working here. So many hours had been used up on Trish, so many whispered conversations and a thousand daydreams.

Today, she didn't feel guilty about it. Today it seemed reasonable to pine for a woman who could kiss her the way that Trish had kissed her. She could indulge herself for this moment, and then go back to trying to push it all down tomorrow. It was exhausting at times, and she needed a break from it.

Trish climbed the small ladder that helped her reach the top shelf, the outline of the muscles in her calves standing out as she moved.

Trish was watching her today too. During some of the rare occasions that June had actually been working, she glanced up to catch Trish in the act of averting her eyes.

June looked back down at her work. She was proofing a hard copy of one of her chapters and scribbling notes in the margins.

"You're doing some corrections?" Trish asked.

June nodded. They didn't often speak while they were at the library, but it wasn't surprising that Trish was talking to her today. It was so quiet that there mustn't be much for her to do.

"I think this chapter is nearly done, but you know when you've looked at something for so long you just can't tell if it's any good anymore? I don't know if it's even at the stage I'd be comfortable giving it to Anne to read."

"I'm no expert when it comes to editing, but if you just need a second set of eyes for grammar and things like that, I'd be happy to look it over?"

June eagerly handed the papers over to her. "Please, just take it. I could use the help. And be kind."

Trish sat on the edge of the desk, close enough that June could reach out and touch her. June looked at Trish's knee, and at the edge of her skirt just above it. She was near enough that she could slide her hand up Trish's skirt and along her thigh, if she wanted to. And she did want to.

Of course, it was far beyond the boundaries of what they had decided. Hugs and hand holding were one thing, something like that was entirely another.

June drummed her fingers on the desk. This would be much easier if Trish had sat in the chair across from her, and June wondered why she hadn't. Moments later, as though hearing her thoughts, Trish moved over there. Trish gestured for June to hand her a pen so that she could alter the position of an apostrophe.

When she was done, Trish looked up at June and smiled.

"This is a really amazing piece of work. You're a great writer. It's just that one thing I corrected, I wouldn't change anything else."

"Please. Do go on," June said.

Trish laughed, shaking her head. "You must know how good this is. If the rest of your book is anything like this, it's going to be wonderful. I can't wait to read it."

"Thank you, really. I appreciate your help."

"Don't mention it," Trish said.

"What are you doing for lunch?" June asked.

Trish shrugged, finally breaking eye contact. "I made too much dinner last night for my family and meant to bring the leftovers, but I forgot. So, did you want to go out? Get a sandwich or something?"

"Seems like a waste. I can run you back home if you really want to have your leftovers?" June said, holding up her helmet. "Quicker than the train, and a car too. You're in Fairfield, aren't you? We could be there and back in no time at all. You never have taken that ride with me."

"There's enough food for two so it's not a bad idea. But I can't take your helmet, what would you use?"

"Oh, I gave Ollie a ride to Max's before I came here, and there's a helmet strapped to the back of my bike. What do you say?"

"It does make sense. Let's go," Trish said.

June mounted her bike, waiting while Trish got on behind her. Trish took the steadying hand that June offered her, though she really didn't need it. She closed her eyes when she was settled in behind June. In the last weeks she'd imagined riding with June like this. Instead of taking advantage of the opportunity she sat slightly back, too nervous to lean in as she remembered June's recent accident. But that was soon forgotten as they weaved in and out of traffic, a smile splitting her face by the time they arrived at her house.

June looked up at the house, eyebrows raised. "Nice place."

Trish showed June around the house, leading her from room to room. She couldn't help noticing that every time June complimented something, an ornament or a painting or the placement of a piece of furniture, it was a change that she had made since Katrina's departure.

Trish heated up the steak with the mushroom sauce that she had made the night before.

"Let's hope this doesn't make it taste like an old piece of leather," she said. June was such a foodie, and Trish wished that she had something more sophisticated to serve her. Her fears disappeared when June tucked in.

"Mmm. You've cooked this just right. The sauce has so much flavor."

"It isn't anything special," said Trish, taking her seat at the kitchen table.

"Sometimes it's the simplest stuff that's the best," June replied.

It was too quiet, no sound but the scraping of June's knife while she cut her steak. Trish suspected that she was the only one who was finding this uncomfortable. June looked at home at the kitchen table, slumped down in her chair. Trish was conscious of the bed in the next room, and the fact that they were alone. They were almost always surrounded by other people. There was no chance of being interrupted or watched now. The thought was dangerous.

"Thanks for inviting me around. Well, I invited myself around, but you know what I mean. It's cool to get to see your house," June said, her toned arms showing as she picked up her glass of water.

Trish jerked her wrist in front of her face and looked at her watch. "That's okay. But you know, I really should be getting back."

"No problem."

This time, Trish moved close to June, settling in snugly behind her. June had given Trish her jacket to wear, and Trish looked down at her leather-clad arms encircling June's waist. She felt like she was stuck inside one of her own fantasies all the way back to the library. She had her arms and legs wrapped around June, her torso tight against June's back. The bike rumbled heavily underneath them. When they stopped at a light June put her hand on Trish's knee, and Trish hugged her more tightly, pressing up against her.

It felt so right; she didn't want the ride to end. Judging by the way that June reluctantly stepped off the bike, she felt the same way. Trish removed the helmet, trying to smooth down her hair where it had come loose.

"That was fun. I can see why you like it so much," Trish said. She unzipped the jacket and gave it back to June.

"Thanks. You know, I'm going to be here the rest of the day. I can give you a ride home if you want."

Trish pushed her hair back behind her ear. "That would be great. It's just that I need to stay back a while after closing and do a few things. It would mean you'd have to wait."

"That's not a bad thing. I can get a little extra work done."

The building emptied out and the doors closed. June heard Trish sending off a couple of library assistants and gathered that it was just the two of them in the building now.

June refreshed her word count and was satisfied at the significant progress she'd made today, which she'd managed to do even with all the distractions. If she kept up this pace, she might even be able to afford to take a couple of days off soon. Maybe Trish would want to hang out, and they could get out of the city on the bike. Trish had seemed to enjoy the ride today. It was a thrilling idea, the two of them out in the mountains somewhere or at the beach, Trish's legs wrapped around her on the way.

June stretched, looking around and wondering how much longer Trish was going to be, when Trish poked her head around a corner.

"I won't be long. I just need to tidy up a few things. Ms. Rose is on tomorrow, and she's very particular about the way we close up."

"I bet she is," June said, and they laughed.

June got up to walk around and stretch her legs. Being here reminded her of a movie she'd watched as a kid, where a bunch of people were locked in a mall for the night. It felt like everyone else in the world had disappeared. It felt like anything could happen.

June located the fiction section in the stacks. She couldn't remember the last novel that she had finished. Maybe she should ask Trish to recommend her something. It never ceased to impress her, how well-read Trish was. The books here were mainly classics and a lot of them were familiar to her, but there were also plenty of titles that she had never cracked open. Now she picked one up and read the first sentence, running her finger over the words.

She didn't hear Trish approaching. She wasn't sure how long Trish had been standing there.

"Are you ready to go?" June asked.

Trish kept opening her mouth and then closing it again, rubbing her hands on her thighs.

"What is it?"

"I'm not sure that it's a good idea anymore," Trish said.

"What do you mean?"

Trish put a hand out, bracing herself on the shelf next to her. "I don't know."

June closed the book and returned it to its place, then moved closer to Trish. She didn't really need to ask. She knew very well why Trish was hesitating, because of what had been between them all day.

"Tell me," June said. She needed to hear her say it.

Trish exhaled. "I'm afraid that if we go on the bike, and I'm close to you again like that, I won't be able to stop myself from inviting you inside when we get home. Which would mean either embarrassing myself if you said no, or doing something we shouldn't if you were to say yes."

June watched her levelly, weighing up her next move.

"Do you really think I'd say no to you?" June said.

"I'm sorry," Trish said.

"It's okay. Listen, do you want me to just go? I can walk out of here right now if that's what you want." When Trish shook her head, June beckoned her closer. "Then come here. Just talk to me."

Trish walked over to June, slowly. They both leaned against the shelves, standing close to one another.

"It would have been a hard yes, for the record," June said. Trish laughed, but it didn't reach her eyes. June lifted a hand and lightly passed it over Trish's cheek.

When she dropped her hand, Trish took it between her own. "I know I must seem very confused. I keep trying to change the rules on you."

June shook her head. "I think we could do with a change in the rules. There's nobody stopping us, is there? Do you want to kiss me again?"

Trish drew deep breaths. Her gaze never moved from June's lips.

"We've done it before. We could always just act like it didn't happen, just like we did today. Whatever we decide is okay is okay. If that's what you want."

"And you would be okay with that?"

"Yes," she lied.

June was so close to pulling Trish toward her, to doing what she knew they both wanted. But Trish was still just looking at her, not moving, and June was starting to wonder if this was worth sacrificing her dignity for. What was she doing? Had she lost her mind?

"Good night, Trish," June said, trying to not let frustration creep into her voice. It wasn't that she was mad at Trish, not exactly. One look at her and the agony she was in made it clear that she wasn't intending to be difficult. A different kind of woman might have just jumped in by now rather than being so worried about the consequences.

June would be okay, she just needed a good long ride around the city to cool down, and time to think about how to stop this from happening again.

As she turned Trish's hand was on her arm, firm and insistent.

"It's okay, Trish. I just need some time to myself," she said, but Trish pulled her around until they were facing one another. In a moment, June's back was against a shelf. The impact was light but June had thrown out an elbow, so the books thudded to the ground.

Trish's hands were on her shoulders now. Their faces were so close together that Trish's breath tickled against her mouth.

June pushed the hair back from Trish's face and pressed her lips softly to Trish's forehead, then her cheek, and then finally came to her lips. She felt Trish's mouth open to hers with a shuddering sigh.

They kissed slowly. This time the privacy meant they could indulge themselves in a way that they hadn't before. Trish pressed against her, so close that there was no space between them at all, June's back pushing against the shelves. Trish's hands rested lightly on her waist.

June took her hand and ran it from Trish's hair, down the length of her lean body. As she did it, Trish kissed her harder, stabbing her tongue into June's mouth, the kiss transforming from soft and sweet to something more erotic.

It was a dance, the pressure between them moving back and forth.

Trish took a fistful of June's hair in her fingers and moved her head back to kiss June's neck, as June moved against her. There was no sound but her own breath, fast and loud. Trish's soft tongue licked at her neck, wet heat on her skin.

Words came to June's lips and died there, because as intimate as this was she should not risk making it more so. She wanted to say that she had wanted to kiss Trish since they met, that she loved kissing her so much. For now, she had to be content to focus on the sensations. Trish was kissing her neck, pulling down the front of her shirt to place her mouth on June's collarbone.

June's head was thrown back, her mouth open. She let Trish take the lead, knowing that this all had to be her decision. Trish kissed her way back up June's neck, her breath hot against June's ear.

June reached out and gently took hold of Trish's face in her hands. "Just a sec," she said. "Can I?" She loosened Trish's hair from its bun, running her fingers through it. Trish closed her eyes, her lips parting slightly. June ran a finger along Trish's lower lip, across the softness of it.

They stared into one another's eyes. June thought she might be able to see fear in Trish's face again and she put her hand against Trish's cheek gently.

"Are you okay?"

Trish nodded, staring at June's lips. They came together again, their kiss open-mouthed and fierce.

Trish's hand inched downward to lay on June's breast, and June pushed softly against her hand, arching her back. Then they were standing holding one another, their kisses stopped for a moment as Trish's hand caressed June and June sighed against her.

They really should leave, because if they didn't cool it down they were going to do things that really should not be done here. The thought had barely crossed her mind before she was throwing it away, closing the door on it so she wouldn't have to look at it.

They were joined again, their kisses hard one moment and soft the next. June took Trish's head in her hands and tasted her mouth, intoxicated by it. June could not remember why they were not supposed to be doing this. The smell of Trish's hair made her want to bury her face in it, but she settled for running her fingers through it.

Trish pushed her hand up June's top and touched her over her bra, caressing the shape of her breast.

Still it didn't seem to be enough for Trish. She pulled down the cup, sliding her fingers over June's skin, feeling the weight of her breast in her hand, and it was lovely and it made June gasp, but still it was not enough.

Trish slid her hand down and cupped June between her legs over her jeans, holding her hand there. June's hand, trembling, lay over hers. Their faces were close to one another's, their foreheads pressing together. June's hips jerked forward, and she gripped Trish's hand tightly, rubbing it against her pelvis until Trish pressed her fingers down harder. Trish flicked her tongue over June's lower lip, then reached for the buckle of June's jeans.

There was a loud whirring from downstairs, far away, and it was a measure of how far gone they both were that for a moment it seemed that they were both considering ignoring it. Trish pulled her hand away.

"What's that?" June said breathlessly.

"Shit. Vacuum, I think. The cleaner," Trish said.

"Oh," June said. "What do we do?"

Trish's eyes were darting around. "I think if you go down the back stairs you'll be able to avoid being seen. And I'll go and say hello to them like I normally would. Okay?"

"Yes, I can do that," June whispered. She wanted Trish to ask her to wait outside, but she could see that it was out of the question.

"Will I see you tomorrow for coffee?" June asked.

"Yes, yes, of course," Trish agreed.

While she grabbed her things, June could hear Trish exhaling, pulling herself together, and straightening up her clothes. Trish bent to pick up the books that had been knocked from the shelves. June stood and watched Trish while she pulled her hair back into a messy bun. Her fingers ached to touch Trish again.

CHAPTER TWELVE

Trish sat with her bag clenched between her fingers, her legs jogging up and down while the carriage rumbled around her. The way she acted this evening was completely out of character. She was shocked at her recklessness.

If things had taken a different course, Trish might have lost her job. All it would have taken was for the cleaner to have started on a different floor. She could almost see the cleaner's shocked face in her mind. It would have been so humiliating.

There was nobody else to blame. Though June had been a willing participant, and in fact Trish had to stop herself from thinking about just how wonderfully willing she had been, Trish had been the one to instigate it all. She was also the one who'd escalated things. When she searched herself to try and understand why she had behaved like that, she kept bumping up against the answer. She had never felt quite this way.

It wasn't like she had never been strongly attracted to a woman before. That had happened plenty of times, yet never with this intensity. Trish had been working so hard to control it, and every time she was around June she failed.

Trish crossed her legs, glancing around at the bored faces of her fellow commuters. Why did she feel like people could see inside of her, even though nobody was even looking at her? Her face was hot, and she pressed a hand to her cheek.

Katrina's sudden return to her life must be contributing to all this. Their relationship had been the defining one of her life. These past months had forced her to take a good hard look at that relationship, and a lot of what she saw made her uncomfortable. It was only now that she really let herself analyze what their sex life had been like. At the time, she had thought of it as being good enough, and had rationalized any problems away. Looking back with clearer eyes she couldn't remember it ever being more than just okay.

Katrina liked to be the one to initiate sex, and Trish had picked up early that she didn't like it at all if Trish took the lead. They had settled into unsatisfying patterns early in their relationship, and once they were set Trish hadn't known how to change them. She hadn't even known how to talk about it with Katrina.

June didn't have the same problem with Trish being forward. Trish was just inches away from slipping her hand down June's pants and June's hand pressing down on hers made it clear that it was what she wanted. Trish put her head in her hands. June may have been able to forgive her after the party and that kiss, for the way she had pushed the boundaries of their agreement, but Trish wasn't confident that she would keep being so understanding when it wasn't in the heat of the moment and she had time to think about it.

Trish hoped she was wrong. She had to take June at her word, it was all she could do. June said that they could pretend that it had never happened. It was the only way that Trish could imagine they would still be able to maintain their friendship. They would have to wipe the slate clean between them, and try to return to a time when they didn't know what it was like to kiss one another.

It felt like madness, but she hoped that it would work.

* * *

As she approached the coffee cart, June had no idea what to expect. She arrived early to try and gain some control. Her plan was ruined, because Trish was already standing to the side of the cart, looking down at her phone.

June's stare swept up and down Trish. The blue knit sweater clung to her, showing off her curves. June had been touched the day before, but she hadn't had the chance to reciprocate. She wanted to run her hands over the front of that sweater, and push her hands underneath.

"Hey," June said.

Trish jumped and dropped her phone into her handbag. "Good morning."

"How was your night?"

"Oh, fine, I spoke to Leigh on the phone and got a few chores done. Can I get a latte please? I can only sit for a minute this morning, I was hoping to start early so I can finish early today. Leigh needs me to come and do a dress fitting thing. There's always something with her."

"Right," June said. Trish's rapid speech sent her a clear message, that she was to stay away.

They sat down on the steps, Trish putting space between them as they took their places.

"Do you have a lot of work to do today?" Trish asked.

"Mainly revisions. I'm not happy with some stuff at the beginning. Sometimes I wonder if I'll ever finish this thing."

"Of course you will."

Trish fiddled with the lid of her coffee cup. Her nails were cut short and covered in clear polish, and her fingers were long. Only yesterday, they'd been on June's breasts.

"How is your sister, anyway?"

"She's good," Trish said.

June stared out at the quad. She couldn't understand why Trish was acting so ashamed of what they'd done. They'd gone against their agreement, but why should they take that so seriously anyway? It had always been flimsy.

"Well, thanks for meeting me," Trish said, standing up abruptly and clutching her bag in front of her. Her knuckles were white where they gripped the strap.

"No worries. I'll see you later," June said.

June stayed on the steps, Trish hurrying away from her. She had allowed herself to hope for too much. As she lay in bed the night before, she'd imagined the intimacy they'd shared bonding them, making them able to talk properly. She'd even thought about joking around about how close they'd come to being caught. If they could laugh about it, it might break any tension.

As soon as Trish had started talking, June knew that a joke would never land. Trish was just meeting June to be polite. She really didn't want to be there.

It was what June deserved. The idea of their romantic friendship was ridiculous, and June had always known it. She was pathetic for proposing it to begin with. There was no point in being upset with Trish, not when Trish had made it so clear that she didn't see June as a serious prospect. Trish wasn't the first person in the world who wanted to have her cake and eat it too. Before they kissed in the library June had told Trish to do just this, had practically given her an instruction manual in how to treat June badly.

Trish's attitude was painful, but there was nothing more painful than her own willingness to keep exposing herself to it.

* * *

Trish had always been a prolific list maker. There were lists clipped to her fridge, for recipes she wanted to try or improvements she wanted to make for the house. There was always at least one to-do list crisply folded into her purse, in a compartment she reserved for that purpose. The natural thing to do when she was having difficulty with making decisions was to make a list of pros and cons.

This situation warranted lists, a lot of them. Trish couldn't come to a decision about what to do about either Katrina or

June. She couldn't even decide whether she should see Katrina for dinner.

Trish sat at her dining table, spreading a couple of pieces of paper in front of her. She would dedicate one page to the pros and cons of seeing Katrina, and another to the pros and cons of pursuing something more with June.

For the dinner with Katrina there were a few things in the positive column—for example, that it might give her a sense of closure. They hadn't talked in a long time and she still had so many questions. Trish wrote that she owed it to Katrina, and to herself, because they had spent so much time building a life together. The negatives she wrote down were that spending time with Katrina would likely only confuse her more, and that being together might make her feel locked into more dates. She wasn't sure that she wanted that.

The list about June was more difficult. The first thing Trish thought of was their mutual physical attraction, and she flashed back to their encounter in the library as she wrote the words. She added the things they had in common (subdivided into things like values and taste in books), and the fact that they had so much fun when they were together. Trish wrote down that she liked talking to June.

Under the negative heading, Trish wrote about their age difference, and the instability in June's life. There was her lack of a full-time job and her odd hours. Trish couldn't imagine spending a lot of time with June's friends aside from Ollie, so she wrote that down too.

The list was growing, and Trish hadn't covered the thing that scared her the most.

"Not a serious person about relationships," she wrote neatly. The whole romantic friendship thing had always been a game for June, and Trish guessed that she was open to all kinds of games when it came to relationships. June might play around on her when she got bored, or she might not even want to be together as a proper couple in the first place.

Something told her that she and June might have very different ideas about what a relationship would even look like.

By the end the cons outweighed the positives, but it didn't seem like a true reflection of how she felt. Maybe there were some things that couldn't be captured by a list.

She needed to gather more information. It wouldn't hurt to see Katrina and hear her out. It was important that she deal with the Katrina situation first, because the outcome of that would determine where things went with June.

Trish laid the pieces of paper on top of one another and tucked them into a folder. She'd have to add to them over the coming weeks, because she didn't know how she was going to make any decisions otherwise.

On Friday morning, Trish chose her clothes carefully. She decided on an outfit that she had purchased after the breakup, a black-and-white dress that was suitable for work but that was nice enough for a restaurant too. She had to prove to Katrina that she was doing just fine without her.

It had been almost a week since the thing with June in the library. They were still getting together most mornings for coffee, and June never tried to raise the subject. Trish was uncomfortable in the beginning; the first day they'd seen one another she'd been so nervous that she hadn't stuck around for long. Once she'd been assured that June wasn't going to say anything, things just felt normal again.

Trish even allowed herself to wonder if something like that could happen again, if the conditions were right. Thinking it made her feel guilty, but no amount of guilt could make her stop wanting June.

As usual, Trish clocked where June was working for the day, in one of her favorite quiets spots on the first floor by a reading room. It was always easy to tell if June was having a good day or a bad one. Sometimes Trish would see her slumped down in her chair like a surly teenager, picking away at her laptop slowly. Other days she would be sitting rigidly in the chair with her fingers flying over the keyboard, her face a mask of blissful concentration. Right now, June wasn't typing at all. She had a sheet of paper in front of her and her chin propped upon her hand, deeply satisfied.

"It's going well, is it?" Trish asked.

"I think I've really nailed this section," June said, the light catching her eyes as she looked up at Trish. It brought out the color more than usual.

"Your modesty never ceases to amaze me."

June gestured toward a nearby chair. "Come, read it. Enjoy my cogent argument. I always know it's good when I can imagine Anne calling it cogent."

"Or astute. That's a good one," Trish said. She lowered herself into the chair, pulling it into the table across from where June was sitting, and took the pages from her.

"Oh yes, I sure do love being called astute."

Trish disliked academic writing that made the work too hard to follow, and she hated big words that were only there for the author to show off. But there was a beautiful clarity in June's writing. When she was finished, Trish held up the pages.

"I can confirm that this is both cogent and astute." June grinned at her. "No, seriously, I can see why you're pleased. This is fantastic. It ties everything up so well, really brings it all together."

Trish jumped when she felt the warm length of June's leg press up against hers. It was the first time June had touched her all week. They were joined from ankle to knee, and Trish lightly pushed her leg back against June's.

She flicked back through the writing to read out a couple of sentences that she particularly liked. Trish had come to love the sensation of June watching her, hooked on the steady gaze that made her feel like she was pretty. At times, she caught herself performing for June, doing little things she wasn't conscious of at first, like flicking her hair or sitting in a way that would flatter her figure. It would embarrass her if anyone else ever noticed, but she loved the way June responded to her.

"Can you read out some more?"

"Oh, you really are pleased with yourself, aren't you?"

June looked back at her, not smiling anymore. "It's not that. I think you have a sexy voice. I like hearing you."

Slowly, Trish cleared her throat and then began to read. She put the paper down on the table so that it wouldn't show that her hand was shaking.

"Thank you. Is there anything you noticed that needs work?" June asked quietly.

Trish shook her head and pushed the papers back across the table. "Not a thing. Would you like to have lunch with me to celebrate?"

June pulled her legs away. "I'd love to, but I might just grab a sandwich to go. I should get across to class."

Trish tried to cover her disappointment. Their lunches together, and the opportunity they afforded to talk at length, always made her days so much brighter. They hadn't had lunch this week.

"What are you doing this weekend?" June asked, standing to pack her things.

Trish hesitated, unsure of whether to reveal that she had plans with Katrina. She should have thought about this, because keeping quiet about it now would make her feel like she was lying. Dinner with Katrina was literally the only engagement she had for the weekend.

"I'm meeting Katrina for dinner," Trish said. June paused, a pen between her fingers. She slowly tucked it into her bag.

"I didn't realize the two of you were still friends."

"We're not really. She just came over last weekend, asked me if I could meet her for dinner," Trish said. When June remained quiet, Trish talked on. As it came spilling out of her she realized how much she'd been needing to talk to someone about it. "She wants to talk about things actually, about us. I feel like I should hear her out. It's very strange, I never expected it."

"Oh. Right," June said. She didn't meet Trish's eye as she pushed her laptop into her backpack.

"So, um, yes. We're going to a place in Toorak. What about you, what are you doing?" Trish said. June was not receptive to this conversation, and she wished she hadn't said anything. She didn't know why she'd thought she could.

June shrugged. "Not much. I'm working on Sunday night. I have a game tomorrow night."

They had talked about Trish coming along to other roller derby games, but June clearly didn't intend to invite her, and Trish didn't want to invite herself. Had June been about to invite her, before she'd screwed everything up?

"Well, good luck. I hope you win again," Trish said.

"Thanks. Have a good weekend."

"You too."

"You look really nice, by the way," June said. "I like your dress."

In the moment before she moved to leave, June finally stopped avoiding eye contact, and her glance felt like a punch in the stomach. There was so much pain in her expression in that moment that Trish wanted to hold her, to soothe her, but she had to let June pass.

Trish looked down at herself, at her dress. She wished she'd never worn it.

CHAPTER THIRTEEN

Katrina took Trish's arm as they walked, guiding her around a puddle. They'd parked the next street over from Ryori, a Japanese restaurant in Toorak. Trish rarely visited the affluent neighborhood and she looked around warily, wishing she'd taken the initiative and picked the place herself.

She wondered what June would think. She looked up at the sign over the door, doubting that June would have anything good to say about somewhere so pretentious. When Trish checked the menu online, the dishes were crazy expensive.

"I feel really underdressed," Trish said.

"I already made a reservation, it's really hard to get into this place on a Friday night!"

"I know, but…"

"You're going to love it. And you look perfect, you're going to be the most beautiful woman in there."

Trish let Katrina open the door for her. When they were shown to their table, Katrina pulled out a chair for her, despite the fact the hostess was about to do it.

"Should we get a bottle of red?" Katrina asked, scanning the menu.

They always ordered a bottle of wine of Katrina's choosing. Trish had already decided that she was going to be paying for her own half of the meal. Katrina would order the most expensive wine she could and then insist on paying for it.

She wasn't in the mood for wine, anyway. "Actually, I think I'll have a beer."

Katrina laughed. "Since when do you drink beer?"

Trish ignored the question, reading over the descriptions on the beer list until she found a wheat one that looked good.

They made small talk about mutual acquaintances until their food arrived. She was already tipsy from her beer, enough to ask Katrina the questions she'd been rehearsing in her mind all week.

"So, what's this all about, Katrina? I don't understand why we're here."

There was something affected about the way Katrina wiped her mouth with her napkin, took a deep breath, and held Trish's hand. It was clear to Trish that she wasn't the only one who'd been rehearsing.

"We were both young when we got together, weren't we?"

"Not that young. We weren't exactly teenagers."

Katrina shook her head. She had always been easily irritated when Trish disagreed with her, and even the small correction bothered her. Trish might have been more assertive with her earlier if she had known how good it would feel.

"Okay, maybe we weren't that young. But young enough that I still had a lot of questions, felt like I hadn't experienced things. I guess I got curious, and I wondered what else was out there."

Somewhere inside she'd always known that Katrina felt that she wasn't enough, but it was hard to hear her say the words aloud. Trish searched Katrina's face, finding nothing there. Katrina wasn't even aware that she'd said anything hurtful, and she just kept on talking.

"It was immature of me. But if I was going to commit to you for the rest of my life, I needed some time on my own to be sure of what I wanted."

Trish looked over Katrina's shoulder, avoiding her eye. "You weren't on your own for very long, though, were you?"

"I didn't plan that, it just happened. It was a mistake."

"Seemed pretty serious to me."

"Things aren't always as they appear, you know that. Listen, I can see now that taking a break at all was a selfish thing to do, and that I should have trusted my instincts in the first place. You and I were always supposed to be together. I think we're supposed to be together now."

Katrina was leaning forward in her chair, and Trish subtly leaned away from her. Katrina's hand was clammy on top of hers, and Trish wondered if she was nervous for once. Katrina had always been able do things without breaking a sweat that Trish would never dream of.

"I want us to be together. I want to make up for the time I made us lose. Maybe we could even have some conversations about starting a family."

Trish pulled her hand out from under Katrina's and picked up her beer glass. Katrina had always been good at persuading her to do things. She had a knack for talking Trish into big purchases that she wasn't sure about, or for guiding her toward clothes she wanted to see Trish wearing. Now Trish felt herself once again drawn into Katrina's version of reality, losing grip on things that she had been so sure of just moments before.

"I'm not sure what I want to be honest with you," Trish said. "This is all really confusing."

"Then don't decide right now. You don't have to be sure. I'm just asking for a second chance, just to see what happens."

"What would that look like? What does a second chance mean to you exactly? You make it sound so much simpler than it actually is, like you think we can just pick up where we left off."

"I don't think that at all. I think of it as a fresh start, where we get to know one another again."

"How can we really have a fresh start after everything that's happened? How could you be so sure about breaking up and then be so sure about this too?"

"I just am. It's simple to me, really."

"Lucky you," Trish said.

Katrina grasped her hand again. "It's okay, Trish. We can make this simple. Let's just try. We could just see one another a couple of times, feel things out. Go on another date or two. You can call it off whenever you want."

"Of course I could."

"I didn't mean it like that. I just meant I'm not expecting you to make any big decisions any time soon. Trish, I'd do anything for a second chance."

Trish stared down at the table. There was a huge part of her that was already sure she didn't want to go down this road. Still, she couldn't imagine cutting down Katrina's hopes over dinner. This had been so important. It felt important now to at least give it all some serious consideration.

She nodded. "Okay. Just to see."

* * *

When June got home, she crawled onto her mattress, not bothering to turn the lights on. She stared into the dark. Trish had indicated so many times that she wasn't interested in a relationship, and June ignored it. Even when she had been trying to be a good friend, she had held out hope that Trish would change her mind one day. It had been unthinkable that she wouldn't.

How could two people have so much chemistry with one another, and not act on it? How could they be so in tune with one another and not explore it further? Maybe she had deluded herself, but June kept coming back to the way Trish looked at her and everything that had happened between them lately. She still couldn't believe that she might be wrong about how they fit together. She knew in her heart that Trish felt it too.

June had no idea what Katrina looked like, but her brain conjured up an image of a beautiful woman. They would be kissing right now, or worse. The thought of anyone else's hands on Trish made her stomach turn over. As her ex-girlfriend, Katrina must know Trish's body better than anyone else. If Trish was still in love with Katrina, which June had always suspected that she was, then June could never compete with that.

She put a pillow over her face and groaned into it. Trish had pushed and pulled her from the day they met, and June had finally reached her limit.

Eventually she changed her clothes and got under the covers, drifting asleep without showering or eating dinner. She left her bedroom door wide open, and when she woke up Ollie was in bed next to her.

She rolled over and looked at him. Harsh sunlight was coming through the curtains, making it impossible for her to open more than one of her eyes.

June groaned senselessly.

He snapped awake and rolled toward her. "What's wrong with you, baby girl, are you sick?"

"What are you talking about?"

"I said, grumpy Gus, are you sick? I came home and your door was open, but half the lights were on. Plus, I peeked under the covers and saw you're wearing that hideous shirt you always wear when you're depressed."

June looked down at it. She had a lot of bed shirts, but the one she was wearing was ripped under the sleeve.

"You pay too much attention to my clothes. It doesn't mean anything."

"Bullshit. What happened?"

June sighed and rubbed her face. "I haven't even had coffee yet so you're pushing it, but okay. Some stuff happened with Trish."

"What kind of stuff?"

June pulled the blanket over her head, shutting out the world for just a moment, then pulled it back down again. She stared up at the ceiling. "We fooled around."

"You did?"

"We did. And it wasn't supposed to be a big deal, but I thought we were getting closer anyway. Then she tells me that she's seeing her ex again. She told me like I was just a girlfriend, you know? Like I'm just there to listen to her problems and not have any feelings about anything."

"That's really not okay. I know I just met her, but I didn't think she'd do something like that."

"I don't know, I guess things have gotten pretty blurry between us. There's something else I haven't told you about."

"What is it?"

June threw her arm over her face. "You're going to think it's so dumb."

"You know I'm not here to judge. Come on, tell me."

"Well, we made kind of this pact…we were talking about my book topic and we thought it would be funny, I guess, to see if we could have that kind of relationship."

"A romantic friendship?"

"Yep. We agreed we could be physical with each other as long as we didn't take it too far, but then we did anyway. I've been so stupid, Ollie, I just wanted to be close to her. I thought I could handle it, but I couldn't. She doesn't want me."

Ollie put an arm around her, and she moved so that she could rest her head on his chest.

"Where do you want things to go from here?"

"There's nowhere it can go, I've finally figured that out. I've just got to watch while she gets together with Katrina, I guess."

"That sounds really horrible."

"What do you think I should do?"

Ollie sighed, stammered, and still didn't say a word.

"I promise I'm not going to get mad," June said. "I know what I've done. I really want you to tell me what you think."

"Okay. I know what it's like, you're totally into this girl, I get it. But I don't think she's ever going to see you any differently. You're right, you'll just have to watch her get back together with her ex. If you don't tell her it's not okay she's just going to keep doing it to you. And, um, as for the romantic friendship thing, I think it's for the best if I don't say what I think about that."

"Please don't," June said. "So? You think I should do what?"

"There's two things that you can do. You can keep suffering in silence and let her keep hurting you, or you can go on a Trish cleanse. Stop spending time with her, definitely don't do any of this weird hand-holding shit, just go back to being friendly acquaintances at the library. It'll hurt but eventually you'll get her out of your system."

"Or the other option is I could talk to her, tell her how I'm feeling?"

"You've tried that. She knows how you feel."

June let the words sink in, allowing herself to really comprehend the awfulness of it. "You're right. I have. It needs to be the cleanse. No more coffee dates, no more lunches. Tear up that stupid piece of paper. I don't even owe her an explanation really, do I?"

Ollie grabbed her hand and squeezed it. "You don't owe her anything. Only talk to her as much as you want to. You need to look after yourself."

Now that a decision was made, June didn't feel much better. It was one thing to determine that she needed to keep her distance, quite another to follow through. She was going to have trouble staying away from Trish, that much was obvious. This time, she needed to stick to her guns.

* * *

Trish didn't know who to turn to, not when everyone in her life had an agenda. Both of her parents would tell her to get back together with Katrina if they knew there was any chance of a reconciliation. If Leigh were to find out, she'd beg Trish to run for the hills. When it came to people at work, Trish still didn't know anyone well enough to talk to. She was friendly with a lot of people there, but none of them were really friends. None of them knew anything about her personal life.

It wasn't just Katrina that she needed to talk about. She felt sick about that look June had given her.

Trish considered calling June over the weekend, but she couldn't think of a convincing pretext to do it. She didn't know exactly what she wanted from June, but it would be enough to know that they were okay and that June wasn't mad at her. Instead, she forced herself to wait until they could see one another again. Just the thought of seeing June's face lifted her up. She needed a break from all this confusion.

On Monday morning, she checked her lipstick in her compact before leaving her handbag in the staff room. No matter how many times she saw June, and how friendly they became, she still felt nervous every time they had plans to meet. June always looked so good without appearing like she was trying.

Trish checked her phone as she walked toward the doors. There was a text message from June.

"Hey, Trish. I'm running late and won't have time for coffee today. Sorry for the short notice."

Trish put her phone back in her pocket. She bought a coffee for herself anyway. Surely it was only a coincidence, although she couldn't ignore the fact that she had never known June to be late. Even on days when she'd worked at the bar and only managed a few hours' sleep, June was always there right when she said she would be. Trish had been taking that for granted.

When she started work, Trish kept one eye trained on the entrance, afraid that she would miss it when June came inside. June arrived while Trish was serving a student at the loans counter. Trish looked over the student's shoulder, nodding toward June. June smiled and waved at her like she would any other day. It was only paranoia that had made her worry earlier.

The moment Trish had the opportunity to leave her post, she found where June was working, so that she could say hello properly. She wasn't in any of her usual spots, instead set up in a busy corner by the technology-related texts.

"Good morning," Trish said.

June was sitting with her back to Trish, and Trish noted with alarm the way her shoulders hunched a little when she spoke. Still, when she turned in her chair, June met her eyes with a smile. As usual, her gaze slid down Trish's body, and as always Trish pretended to not notice, enjoying every bit of it.

"Morning. How was your weekend?"

"Not bad," Trish replied. She grasped for something to fill the silence that followed. "How was your game?"

"We won," June said.

"That's great. Congratulations."

June hadn't risen from her chair or even properly turned around, and Trish touched her shoulder as she congratulated her. But June didn't put her hand on Trish's like she normally would. Trish dropped her hand, which suddenly felt weighted down, useless.

Trish was beginning to understand that she was going to have to give an explanation about Katrina. She would have to broach the topic if she wanted to clear the air. It wouldn't work to do it now. Trish wanted privacy, and time to think of what to say.

"Would you like to have lunch with me today?" Trish asked.

June picked up her pen, rolling it between her thumb and forefinger. She was facing away from Trish again. Trish was sure of what June's answer was going to be.

"I'm sorry, there's no time. One of my friends at the bar called in sick and I'm covering her shift. I start at noon."

"That's too bad."

June acknowledged her statement with a dip of her head.

Trish had too much pride to try to confirm a coffee date for the next morning, not when it was obvious that June would make up another excuse to avoid her.

"Well, I'll leave you to your work then."

"Cool, I'll see you later," June said, already writing something in her notebook.

June looked down at the scribbled words, not really seeing them. It felt cruel to treat Trish this way, but Ollie was right. Trish knew how she felt about her, and she had no respect for those feelings. Together they had gotten deeper and deeper into trouble, and June had to be adult enough to dig herself back out.

It didn't matter anyway. It wouldn't take long for Trish to file June back into her place as an experiment. June had only ever been something different for Trish to try, just a way for her to kill time until she got back to her real life. If it hadn't been Katrina, some other woman would have come along, someone that Trish would think was good enough for her.

Just now June had felt Trish's brief touch like a caress and wanted more. The awareness of her standing so close was enough to drive June crazy. June wanted to turn and grab her, to pull her onto her lap and kiss her neck. There was so much that she wanted to do, and it worried her how little she cared about the consequences when it came down to it. She had to keep reminding herself that her dignity was worth more than the brief satisfaction she would get from touching Trish again.

June didn't know how she was going to ride this out, but at least she had just taken the first step.

CHAPTER FOURTEEN

"What are you thinking about?" Katrina asked.

Slowly, Trish refocused on Katrina's face. Trish had no idea how long it had been since she'd zoned out, but it was some time after Katrina had started talking about her job.

"Nothing," Trish said, digging a fork into her food. "This pasta is great."

This time they were at an Italian restaurant Trish liked, but she wasn't enjoying herself any more than she had during their last date. Trish couldn't stop ruminating about everything that had happened in the last week, trying to figure out if there was any chance that June would ever stop freezing her out. June still smiled at her, but their conversations were reduced to small talk. She was always rushing out of the library, as though she was desperate to be anywhere else.

This morning, Trish finally gathered up the courage to approach June properly. Trish found a reason to walk past June, and after checking to see that nobody was around, she stood nearby until June noticed her.

"Hey, Trish," June said, barely looking up from her laptop. The disinterested tone was a knife in the chest.

"I'm sorry to interrupt, but can I ask you something?"

June looked back at her, still not taking her fingers from the keyboard. She nodded at Trish to signal that she should go ahead, or maybe she was just telling Trish to hurry up.

"Are you okay?" Trish asked.

"Sure, I'm fine."

Trish stood before her, unmoving. June was looking right through her, and it was so unnerving that she didn't know what to do.

"I'm sorry but I'm really busy here," June said, gesturing at her laptop.

"No, I'm really sorry," Trish said quickly. "I shouldn't have interrupted you, sorry about that."

As she walked away, Trish swallowed down the lump in her throat. Not only did she miss June desperately, she hated that June didn't respect her anymore. Now that the feeling was gone, she realized how much more confident and happy she was while she was spending time with June.

For one thing, June talked to her like they were on the same intellectual level. She sought out Trish's opinions on literature and valued her skills as a researcher.

The same could not be said for Katrina. It was only their second date since reconnecting, and already the familiar condescension was creeping back in. When Katrina asked her for more information about her new job, she only listened for a minute before she jumped back into talking about herself again.

"And what have you been up to lately? You said you went out with a friend?" Katrina finally asked, after a drawn-out story about one of her cases.

"No, I went to a party. At my friend June's place," Trish replied. "She teaches at the university."

"Oh, she's a professor?"

Trish shrugged. "I watched her play roller derby and then went to a party at her place."

Despite everything that had happened since then, the memory of it brought a smile to her face.

"Roller derby. Isn't that the game where they play on skates? She sounds interesting, I'd love to meet her one day."

Trish shrugged again. Even if she decided to keep seeing Katrina, she couldn't imagine a scenario in which a meeting between June and Katrina could ever happen.

While Katrina drove her home, she alternated between tapping her fingers on the steering wheel and playing with her hair. As they pulled into the driveway, Trish quickly unbuckled her seat belt, commenting on how lovely the restaurant had been. She couldn't wait to be alone again.

Katrina's hand was on her shoulder. "Trish?"

Trish turned and Katrina leaned toward her. Trish put out a hand, resting it on Katrina's chest to stop her from coming any closer.

"I really can't do that right now," Trish said.

"That's okay, I understand," Katrina replied. "I had a really nice night. I'll call you?"

"Sure," Trish said. Katrina's voice was tight, no matter how she said all the right things. Trish hadn't asked for any of this.

The car idled in the driveway while she unlocked the door, fumbling the key in the lock under Katrina's stare.

The idea of them kissing felt so wrong; stopping it had been reflexive. There was an absence of passion when she thought about kissing Katrina, and even of warmth. Trish had not felt the barest stirring of desire when she'd seen Katrina looking at her like that. When compared to how she felt when June came near her, it was like the difference between ice and fire. She hunched her shoulders tight until the car was gone and she was safely inside.

* * *

Trish kept her eyes closed while she sat on the train, breathing deeply to try to calm her anxiety. After the date with Katrina she spent the rest of her weekend exercising and reorganizing her closet. None of her self-help strategies were working. On Saturday night, she restlessly watched a movie, and then pulled out her pros and cons lists to look over them. She was hoping to add to them after seeing Katrina again, but she couldn't face thinking about it too deeply. She eventually dumped them on the entry table, where she usually put things when she was on her way to throwing them out.

Trish was so nervous about seeing June again that she'd barely slept. She both dreaded it and needed it. When she thought about the way June had been with her on Friday, she knew that she had used up her last chance to talk about what was going on between them. How many times could she approach June before she started to look pathetic? How long would it be before June would say something that might really hurt her?

When June entered the room, her step slowed slightly as she saw Trish. Trish couldn't remember the last time June had smiled at her. June had never looked more beautiful, in blue jeans and a loose black sweater with sneakers. She looked tired, though, as tired as Trish felt.

June walked on. Trish turned away from her, unable to bear any more.

At least Leigh would be coming to the library to visit during Trish's lunch break. She could certainly use the friendly face. Leigh was taking a day off from work for wedding planning and had asked to come in, so that she should finally check out Trish's new workplace.

Trish was at the front counter when she saw her sister, and her spirits lifted just enough to make her smile. She stepped around the counter and enveloped Leigh in a hug. Leigh returned it, looking at her curiously when they pulled away. Trish had never been much of a hugger.

"How's the planning going? Got much done this morning?" Trish asked.

"Good, good. Lots of emailing and phone calls. I wish we had the money to just hire a wedding planner, though. It's all a bit boring."

"Sounds like it."

Trish looked over Leigh's shoulder. June was walking diagonally across the room and giving them a wide berth, avoiding looking directly at them.

"I told you! I told you, you moron!" a student yelled to their friend by the door. Leigh started, throwing a look over her shoulder.

"Jeez you need to pull these kids into line, so loud! Hey, June?" Leigh said.

June paused, wide-eyed. "Hi, Leigh," she said. "I didn't see you there."

Leigh beckoned her over with an urgent wave of her hand, oblivious to June's discomfort. Trish squirmed at the way June came forward with her shoulders hunched up, directing a furtive glance toward Trish.

"I was hoping I'd get to see you here too! We're going out to lunch, please come join us?"

Trish stood quietly on the sidelines, waiting to see what June would do. June's gaze drifted toward her again and Trish looked back at her steadily. Keeping her expression neutral, as though she didn't care, she wanted to send the message that June could do whatever she wanted.

"Thanks, but I should get going, I have to be at work…"

"Oh, come on, we won't be long. You already missed our dinner, I'm going to start thinking you're avoiding me!" Leigh said.

Trish winced. Her sister could be so forceful, but she did it with such a charming smile on her face that people were never offended by it.

"Well, we can't have that," June said.

Leigh clapped her hands together. "Yay. Trish is always going on about how much you know about food, you can pick where we go."

They walked off the campus onto the busy city street, Leigh placing herself in between June and Trish. For once, Trish was glad that Leigh was such a motormouth and that there was no way for anyone else to get a word in edgewise. June guided them onto a tram that they travelled on for a couple of blocks, getting off at a small vegetarian café called Yam Shack, on a busy corner. It was almost full, so the hostess offered a bench seat at the front. The three of them sat side by side facing the window, and once again Leigh took up a position in the middle, acting as a human buffer.

Leigh checked out the menu and nodded. "Trish was right! You know your stuff. Let's get some share plates, shall we?"

"Sure," Trish and June said at the same time.

Leigh insisted that June take charge of the ordering.

"Can we get two serves of the polenta chips, the tempeh meatballs, arancini, and the rainbow salad please," she said, ordering without looking at the menu again.

While they waited for their lunch, both Trish and June prompted Leigh to keep talking about her wedding.

"How are you doing with writing the vows?" Trish said.

"Getting there. Andrew's freaking out about his part, though."

"Are you including quotes and stuff like that?" June asked, looking over toward the kitchen.

"Sure. It's become a bit of a competition between us, but of course I'm not allowed to know anything about his. If I look out and don't see anyone crying, I'll feel like I haven't done my job. Anyway, excuse me for a sec, I've got to go to the bathroom."

June looked over her shoulder again to watch Leigh walk away and then stared straight ahead out of the window. She cleared her throat. Trish crossed and uncrossed her legs.

"Sorry you got roped into coming," Trish said. "You could have said no."

June looked over at her briefly, piercingly. Trish wished that she hadn't spoken.

"Hey, that's really weird."

Trish followed June's finger, pointing straight ahead. When she looked out the window she saw Ms. Rose hand in hand with another woman. They were walking past the café, unhurried and deep in conversation.

"That's Anne with her," June explained. "The one who's helping with my book? I'm sure I told you about her."

"Oh! Yes, you did," Trish said. "They look kind of...close? Could they be sisters or something?"

The two women paused where they were standing, and Anne brushed something from Ms. Rose's face.

June started to laugh uncontrollably, infectiously, and Trish joined her. They caught one another's eye and June laughed harder.

They were still breaking up when Ms. Rose looked right at them. Trish put a hand over her mouth and June smiled and waved, shaking her fingers at the two of them.

"Stop it, that's awful!" Trish said. She grabbed June's fingers to stop her. June met her eye and broke into a smile.

Ms. Rose waved back at them stiffly, and Anne gave a cool nod toward them before they walked on quickly. Trish reluctantly dropped June's hand.

"I just can't believe it! I knew Anne had a partner, but she always just calls her Jodie. Jodie is Ms. Rose! Ms. Rose is Jodie! This is blowing my mind!" June said.

"You're kidding. This is crazy. I never would have guessed in a million years," Trish replied.

Leigh slid back in between them. "What are you two going on about?"

"We just saw the craziest thing."

After lunch, Leigh said goodbye to them outside of the café, making a promise that she was going to send an invitation to her next dinner party through Trish. June thanked her, knowing that she would have a solid excuse in place by the time the invitation came.

It was a shame, because she really liked Leigh. It was only the reason she found it so difficult to say no to coming along today. Leigh was so genuine about wanting her to come to lunch, and it felt unfair to punish her for her sister's sins.

June didn't want to think about the fact that this might all be just another fancy rationalization. She still wanted to spend time around Trish, no matter how much she tried to deny it to herself.

During the walk back to the library together, they barely said a word. June was painfully aware of Trish beside her, the loveliness of her close enough to touch. If she reached out she could take her by the arm, or put a palm to the small of her back. She wondered when she was ever going to stop thinking of Trish that way. June was determined to be patient with herself, to keep riding it out. There was no other option.

June didn't know what she wanted sometimes, but she knew that she found Trish endlessly disappointing. Although her goal was to rid herself of her feelings toward Trish, she still found Trish's reactions to her lacking. With everything June had done to cut her loose, Trish had barely put up a fight. All she'd done was approach June once with a vague question, asking if she was okay. Trish's indirectness annoyed June even more. The half-hearted attempt proved to June that she wasn't really that important to Trish in the first place.

As they were nearing the campus Trish finally spoke to her. "Well, it's going to be weird to see Ms. Rose this afternoon."

"I bet."

"I wonder if she'll say anything to me about it…"

They reached June's bike and Trish stood in front of her, adjusting her glasses.

June could barely look at her. The most painful thing about all of this was the fact that she could not turn off her empathy for Trish. She wished she could soothe Trish and tell her that everything was going to be okay with them, even though she knew that it never would be.

June wanted to ask her things too. She was desperate to know if Trish was getting back together with Katrina. It would hurt to find out that she was, but at least it might help her move on. Throughout the lunch she had hoped Leigh might say something to tip her off, but there had been nothing. For all she knew, Katrina had already moved back in to their house.

"Well, you have a good day," June said.

"Thanks," Trish replied.

June could feel Trish's eyes on her while she got ready to leave, and she rode off without looking back.

Trish went back to work. She wished that she could go back and do it all over again, because she had been so on edge that she had let the precious time slip through her fingers. She let Leigh dominate the conversation and tried to stay out of the way, worried that if she talked too much she would say the wrong thing.

The only time she had felt easy in June's company was when they saw Ms. Rose and Anne. It was odd to think that she had edited herself around Ms. Rose, not wanting her colleague to find out about her sexuality. It never occurred to her that Ms. Rose might be with a woman herself.

Trish went into the stacks in the psychology section, sliding textbooks into their places. It wasn't long before Ms. Rose was at her side, scowling at her.

"Trish, I need to speak to you about something. Can you come with me to the breakroom?"

"Of course."

When they arrived Ms. Rose closed the door behind them, and nobody ever closed the door.

Ms. Rose faced Trish with her arms crossed. "You saw me just now, didn't you?"

"When I was having lunch? Yes, I did," Trish replied.

"I understand that the girl you were with is a protégé of sorts of Anne's? The writer?"

"Yes, that's right."

"I hope I can trust you to be discreet? I'd prefer that my colleagues here don't know my private business."

"Yes, of course," Trish agreed. Though she liked a good gossip session, particularly with her sister, it wouldn't have occurred to her to tell their colleagues at the library about this. With a supportive family, Trish's own coming-out hadn't been that difficult. But even so, she found herself concealing her sexuality during uncomfortable times. If a man in a bar asked her out or a near-stranger enquired about a boyfriend, Trish let them think what they wanted. Ms. Rose's position was understandable. "You know I…I date women, too, so I think I get it…" Trish said.

"Oh. You do, do you?" Ms. Rose said.

"Yes. I don't know why I hadn't mentioned it. I just didn't."

There was that cliché that when someone came out, they were still the same person to those around them. Trish understood the sentiment, but in situations like this it didn't fit. Since this afternoon, Ms. Rose was a different woman to Trish, coming alive with history and a secret life that Trish had never guessed at.

Ms. Rose motioned toward the table and they sat down across from one another. "I don't know why I don't either. It's not a big secret or anything, but I like to keep things separate when I'm at work. I got into the habit a long time ago, and now that times have changed so much I just haven't really gotten out of it. I was never one of those out and proud types."

"That makes sense. Things have changed a lot even in the last ten years or so."

"Anne's the brave one. She always has been. She doesn't care who knows what."

Ms. Rose's cheeks reddened, and Trish reached out to cover her hand with her own. "I'm sure you're brave in your own way too."

"Not that brave. But I can't very well tell people there was no Mr. Rose, now can I? It's far too late for that."

Trish's mouth hung open. "There was no Mr. Rose? I felt terrible for you after you told me about your dead husband. There's no dead husband?"

Ms. Rose burst into laughter. "Oh, I know. It's horrible, isn't it? I'm a miss, but I made up that story when I was really young and now I pull it out for special occasions. That's what people get for asking prying questions!"

She caught Trish's eye, and the glint in hers made Trish burst out laughing too. They sat across from one another, giggling.

CHAPTER FIFTEEN

Trish snapped awake, hyper alert though she was in a deep sleep only seconds before. Something must have woken her.

She heard a sound, footsteps down the hall. She bolted upright.

Somebody was in the house.

Trish scrambled to find her phone to call the police and then realized that she couldn't, because the intruder might hear her voice. There was no lock on her bedroom door. She stared through the dark with her eyes wide, waiting for it to open.

She clutched the phone in her fist. She could send a text to someone, her sister, and ask her to call the police. Trish looked around the room, trying to figure out if there was anything that she might be able to use as a weapon if she needed to.

The front door creaked shut while Trish lay still, her mouth dry and limbs frozen. Living alone, this was her worst fear, the reason why she didn't watch horror movies or read crime fiction.

She strained to catch the stranger's movements, but there were no more footsteps. She let a lot of time tick by before she felt safe enough to get out of bed, tempted to pull the sheets up over head like she was a child hiding from a monster. She crept out of her room, and snuck around the house. She checked the closets and peeked behind doors, even checking under her bed.

Finally, she locked herself in the bathroom and called the police, still too scared to turn the lights on.

"Someone's been in my house, can you please send someone right away?" Trish stammered, the woman on the line patiently taking her information. When the call ended, Trish was alone again, hands shaking as she put down her phone.

She walked from room to room, making sure that all the windows were closed and locked. She looked out of the curtains into the darkness. As she paced through the kitchen, she started at her own reflection in the window.

The police would want to know what had been taken. She checked the shelf under the entry table and rummaged through her handbag to find that her purse was gone. There had been a camera on the top of a bookshelf in the hall and Trish ran her hand over the empty space.

The police arrived, two male officers who looked alike enough that they could be brothers. The taller one chewed gum, looking her up and down when she opened the door.

"No signs of forced entry?" he asked.

"I don't think so. I think they came in and out of the front door."

The other officer, a man with a mustache and sandy-colored hair, pulled the door back open, shining his flashlight across it and revealing the key still in the lock.

"Didn't see that when we came in."

Trish covered her face with her hands. "I keep it under that potted plant over there."

Popping his gum, the officer grimaced. "I'd really advise you against doing that."

"Obviously. I leave it there so my family can drop over whenever they want."

"Well, at least the key is still here, so they won't be coming back," the one with the mustache said.

Putting his hand on his belt, the taller guy nodded. "We'll take a statement and gather some evidence. There's been a few of these aggravated burglaries in the area, I'm sorry to say, ma'am."

By the time they were done, it was two o'clock in the morning. She couldn't imagine going back to sleep.

Trish slapped her phone against her palm, thinking. At any other time, she'd call Leigh and go to her place, but Leigh and Andrew had gone out of town to visit Andrew's parents this weekend. They didn't leave a spare key lying around like Trish did.

She went to call her dad, imagining him in his bed fast asleep, and the groggy state he always woke up in. When she and Leigh were kids, they'd mocked the way he stayed asleep when up on his feet for at least ten minutes. A call in the middle of the night about the break-in would be so disorienting for him. There was always her mother, but she'd been badgering Trish about how neither of them should be living alone. She'd suggested that Trish move in with her, and this would only bolster her argument.

Katrina would come over if she asked, but that was out of the question. They had been on another date earlier that night, a lonely and confusing few hours for Trish. They'd gone to a film that Katrina had chosen and that Trish didn't enjoy. Katrina hadn't tried to kiss her this time, but Trish had been acutely aware of her in the dark, inching closer and closer into her space. When Trish was getting out of the car, Katrina asked to see her again the following night. She hadn't known how to say no.

Trish scrolled through the names in her contact list. There wasn't a single friend that she would feel comfortable imposing on right now. The thought of sitting here alone for the rest of the night was unbearable, even with all the lights on.

She had skipped over June's name. She scrolled back up again, staring at the four letters, index finger hovering over them. Even with June's frostiness toward her lately, just thinking of her made Trish feel better. Given what she knew about June's schedule, it was likely that June would still be awake.

At the lunch with Leigh, the ice had thawed between them. Trish could picture the way June grinned at her when they'd seen Ms. Rose and Anne together. If only she could hear June's voice, Trish would feel safe again. She pressed the call button.

"I haven't woken you, have I?"

"No, I was just leaving work actually," June said, and then Trish could hear the sounds from the street around her. "What's up? Is everything okay?"

Trish pressed her palm to her temple, wishing that she hadn't been so impulsive. This had not been the smartest idea. Still she was instantly comforted by June's voice, and by the feeling that she was so near on the other end of the phone line.

"I'm sorry…I…I just got robbed tonight, someone broke in while I was asleep. I don't mean to bother you, I just wanted to talk to someone."

"I'm coming over. I'll be on my way, as soon as I get to my bike," June said.

"You don't have to do that, everything's okay. I mean, I'm safe. The police have been here. I just really wanted to talk to someone."

"I'll be there in twenty minutes," June replied, and hung up.

Trish's calm was short-lived. She rose and checked the locks on all the doors and windows again. At the sound of an engine on her street, Trish rushed to the front window and twitched aside the curtain, dropping it when the car passed by. Remembering her credit cards, she canceled them while she waited, using her tablet. Thankfully that had been in her room on the nightstand, so they hadn't gotten it.

When a knock sounded on the front door, she jumped. Rising, she re-belted the robe that she had put on over her tank top and boxer shorts. She'd hardly opened the door before June reached forward and hugged her. Trish did not want to let go, feeling so safe and warm in June's embrace.

"Thanks so much for coming, I really didn't expect you to," Trish said as soon as June released her from the too-brief embrace.

"I know you didn't. What did they get?"

"My purse, camera, a few other bits and pieces. Nothing too sentimental, so it'll be fine. I'm so glad they didn't take the car. The keys are right there on the entry table. I don't even care about the stuff, really, I just hate that they were in my house."

"I know what you mean. Ollie and I got robbed a few years ago, but at least neither of us were home at the time."

"I'm so lucky they didn't come into my room. Can you imagine?" Trish shook her head, not wanting to think about it anymore. As they walked inside, they had turned to face one another, and now she moved past June, accidentally brushing against her as she went.

"I thought I might have a glass of wine, try to relax a little. Would you like one?" Trish asked, moving toward the kitchen while June followed behind her.

"Why not?"

Now that she was starting to calm down, it was sinking in that after weeks of feeling completely shut out, June had come running to her when she needed her. Trish reached up toward a shelf to take down two glasses. Maybe this was the beginning of things getting better between them again.

Trish moved to the cupboard where she stored her wine and selected her best bottle, a 2004 red from the Barossa Valley that she had been waiting to open. She placed it on the bench in front of June, who checked the label and whistled.

"This is a good one." June poured each of them a glass, deftly tilting from the bottom of the bottle. "Do you mind if I ask why you called me of all people?"

Trish took the glass from June, their eyes locking. "I hope you don't mind. I would have called Leigh, but she and Andrew are staying with his parents at the beach."

June took a mouthful of her wine. "And Katrina's not here, obviously. I mean, you're alone tonight?"

"No. I was with her earlier, but I didn't want to call her." As soon as the words left her mouth she knew that her instinct to be honest was wrong. She didn't like the way June was looking back at her.

Trish knew that Katrina would have done the same thing as June. She would have insisted on coming over. The difference was that Katrina would have bulldozed her way in, talking over the top of her and making Trish feel silly about the keys being in such an obvious place. June hadn't even asked how the burglars had gotten into the house, and it wasn't because she didn't care. It was just in June's nature to take things as they came.

"So, what are you going to do? Would you like me to take you to a hotel so you can get some sleep, something like that?"

The question conjured illicit images in Trish's mind, a picture of the two of them lying in crisp white hotel sheets. Of course, it wasn't what June meant, but the words were evocative all the same.

"No, thank you, though. I'll go to bed here. I'm getting tired again, I never thought I would. It's funny isn't it, how no matter what happens life just goes on," Trish said. She put her hand over her mouth to stifle a yawn.

June placed her glass down on the counter, the wine unfinished. "I think that's my cue to leave."

"I didn't mean that. I was just saying you don't have to do anything. It's more than enough that you came."

June walked out of the kitchen and Trish followed her. "Why are you going?"

June turned to her. Though she was standing there calmly, her fists were clenched and her nostrils flared. She was coiled and waiting to strike. "Don't call me again. I don't want to hear from you."

"I'm sorry that I mentioned her. Maybe I'm not thinking so clearly, it's three o'clock in the morning and I'm exhausted. Please don't go."

"You know, you're really clueless, Trish. I know you think you're the mature one out of the two of us, but I wouldn't be so sure."

"I know. I know I don't know what I'm doing," Trish said. "I'm sorry, okay? She was here but nothing happened. Nothing is going on between us, I haven't even kissed her."

June didn't answer. Trish met her challenging look, refusing to back down.

Abruptly June reached out and grabbed the belt of Trish's robe, loosening it so that it hung open. Trish was aware of the thin material of her tank top and the bare legs that were revealed and so was June, her gaze scorching a trail.

The fear about the burglary had disappeared, replaced by a terror that June would leave her. From the moment she'd walked in, Trish had wanted June to touch her, though she had not acknowledged the desire to herself until now. Trish took a small step forward, just enough to make it clear that she welcomed whatever June wanted to do.

June put one hand behind her neck and slipped the other inside Trish's robe, coming to rest at her hip. Soon they were standing against one another, as close as two people could be. Trish could feel the sweet softness and the solidity of June, laid against her skin.

June's mouth was on her, kissing her fiercely and deeply, while Trish leaned in. Trish put her hands to June's shoulders, gripping her, still afraid that she would go. The robe slipped off her shoulders and she barely noticed as the cool night air met her skin. June's tongue was in her mouth, teasing hers, knowing just how to make her crazy.

"I'm sorry," Trish said into June's mouth.

There was so much more that she wanted to say, but words didn't feel like they meant much right now.

June ignored it, intent upon unravelling her by pushing her against the wall and melting her with her mouth. Though they had kissed a couple of times now, June had never been aggressive like this, and Trish liked it. June's hips were pushing into her, guided by a subtle rhythm only they could feel. June's soft breasts pressed against hers and Trish pushed forward.

June drew back for long enough to pull Trish's tank top up and over her head, throwing it on the ground beside them. Trish could feel June's hot breath on her skin, the exhalation of air at the exposure of her breasts. June cupped them with her hands, her thumbs running over their peaks, her face a mask of longing. Trish arched into her hands, moaning as June moved down to caress her skin with her tongue.

June raised up and kissed her mouth again, the friction as June's shirt rubbed against her nakedness making Trish ache.

Trish bunched June's hair in her hands, submitting to the kiss once more. Her whole body had been set alight, and any moment she might sink to the ground, her legs no longer capable of holding her up.

June's hands were everywhere while they kissed, and Trish's head fell back against the wall.

"Let's go to my room," Trish said, risking the chance that June might stop and change her mind, but she wasn't sure how much more of this she could take standing up. June looked at her with glazed eyes, and to Trish's relief she nodded.

They made it as far as the next room. Trish was walking ahead, June grasping at her waist, pulling her back and keeping her in place. June stood close behind her and kissed the side of her face, moving Trish's hair so that she could kiss her neck.

Sighing, her legs shaking beneath her, Trish shifted so that their lips joined, openmouthed and kissing hungrily. Trish pushed back into June and they ground against one another.

June's hands were rough on her breasts, but it felt right, and when June took her nipple between two fingers, Trish cried out in pleasure until June did it again. Trish turned in June's arms and they sank to their knees together, June pushing Trish down onto the floor and climbing on top of her.

They kissed where they lay, June's hips thrusting into her more firmly than before, Trish's legs coming around June's waist. June was gentler now, her teasingly light hands running over and over Trish's breasts. June managed to keep kissing her all the while.

"Take off your shirt," Trish said.

"Wait," June said breathlessly.

June caressed Trish with her long fingers through the fabric of her shorts and Trish thought she might come just from that soft pressure. Trish moved her hips up, signaling how ready she was. Then June was fumbling at the waistband, and then there was nothing separating June from her, nothing to stop the deft exploration of her fingers. Trish moaned and grabbed June's face in her hands, and June looked down into her eyes before she bent down to kiss Trish's lips once more.

June's touch was light on her, cautious.

"Please," Trish whispered in June's ear, "fuck me."

It was a phrase she had never said to anyone before, but it was the only thing that expressed the urgency that she felt. June sighed before she did just what she was asked, her fingers sliding inside Trish, Trish rising up to meet her.

June's body rocked against Trish, setting a steady beat that was punctuated by the sound of their breath. Trish's eyebrows knitted together, and she knew that her face must be a vision of fulfilment so deep it read like pain. They paused for a moment, Trish helping June pull her shorts and underwear down her legs so that June could move more freely. June stroked her thumb against Trish's center, and she threw an elbow over her face, almost unable to bear how good it felt.

June kept driving her higher. Trish looked up at June leaning over her, the sight of her beautiful face and its expression only adding to the pleasure. Now and then June would touch her lips to Trish's mouth, or draw a line of kisses along her neck. June moved her hand just the right way, Trish's hips thrusting in time with her movements, their communion going on and on.

Finally, Trish reached a shattering climax. With her fingers, June gathered her up until she was clenched tight all over and she burst into waves. June kept kissing her, slowly withdrawing her hand.

Trish pulled June close, wanting to be held by her, anchored to the ground. It was such an odd feeling to be lying here naked while June was fully dressed.

"What a strange night," she said. June's laughter rumbled against her throat.

The playfulness was short-lived. Trish sat up, pushing June along with her. She tore at the buttons of June's shirt, not caring that she broke one or two of them in the pursuit of finally undressing her. June's pants followed, Trish tugging them down as quickly as she could.

Trish pulled June onto her lap until June was straddling her. Trish looked up into June's face and then up and down June's body, taking in the beauty of it. Trish buried her face in June's perfect curves, capturing a nipple in her mouth and lightly grazing it with her teeth. She dug her fingers into June's hips, holding her steady while she moved her tongue against June's breasts.

Trish took her time, feeling June arch into her mouth, June's hands in her hair.

Trish reached down between them and teased June softly, gently, and the sound of June's ragged breath was loud in her ear. She increased her pressure and June's head threw back. Trish stroked against June with her fingers. Caressing her was like touching velvet. Trish bit her lip at how wet June was under her hand. June's response to her was electric.

June moaned Trish's name softly, her grasp releasing. Her mouth hung open, and her eyes were squeezed shut. She pushed Trish's hand away, as though unable to bear any more.

June clung to her and Trish put her hands around June's shoulders, tenderly holding her.

"I'll take that as a compliment," Trish said.

"Please don't make fun of me."

Trish gripped her tighter. There was so much anger and hurt in June's voice. She pulled back so that she could look into June's eyes. "I would *never* do that. I would never make fun of you. Come with me."

Finally, they reached the bedroom, and they laid down together facing one another. Trish rolled onto her side, propping herself on her elbow and looking down at June. Despite the intimacy they had shared tonight she still didn't know how much she could say, or what she was and wasn't allowed to do.

Trish traced a finger down June's chest, drawing it down to her stomach, and watched as June shivered.

Trish rolled on top, kissing her again. Though neither of them seemed willing to say it, what was transpiring between the two of them was something vital, something that Trish would be unable to put into words in the days following.

For Trish, there was no time or need right now for too much thought. There was a path for her mouth that drew her downward until June lay trembling beneath the stroke of her tongue.

CHAPTER SIXTEEN

Trish's face in repose was even more beautiful than it usually was. She lay on her back with the sheet pulled up over her breasts, revealing her perfect collarbone and the gentle slope of her neck. Her chest rose and fell, the breaths slow and steady.

A lump rose in June's throat. She had to get out of here. She wanted to kiss Trish awake, to feel that intimacy between them again. When Trish was beneath her, looking up into her eyes, she could forget that Trish didn't feel the same way about her.

June moved gingerly away and out of the bed, turning back to be certain that Trish had not been disturbed. In the dawn light, she crept out to the living room and found her clothes, pulling them on hastily before she grabbed her bag. She was swinging it around to her back as she walked past the entry table, and knocked off a folder resting on it. June bent down to pick up the scattered pages. As she did, she saw her name.

June's eyes were faster than her brain. She took in what she was looking at more quickly than she could assess whether she should be reading it.

June couldn't believe what she was seeing. It was a pro and con list all about her. Her rage white-hot, she wanted to go back and shake Trish awake. Instead she shoved the papers back into the folder and put them back where she'd found them.

June figured out how to lock the front door on the inside so that she could pull it shut behind her. Despite the urge to slam it, she managed to close it quietly.

When she reached her bike, she wheeled it down the street so that the noise would not wake Trish, only revving the engine when she had put a full block between herself and Trish's house. She didn't know what she was capable of doing or saying right now if Trish were to wake up and see her.

It was just after six, and the streets were eerily quiet. June rode around the empty streets of Fairfield, zigzagging around the side streets, slowly crossing back over to her home. It was only when she had been out on the road for some time that she gave in to the feelings that had been threatening to break out since the minute Trish had fallen asleep. June had not slept at all. She'd lay there either staring up at the ceiling or at Trish, thinking about what she'd done.

She was ashamed, so much that she didn't know what to do with it.

She had undone the benefits of every bit of the distance she had gained from Trish. Coming to the house had destroyed the mastery that June had been working on gaining over her emotions. She now understood the extent of her feelings for Trish. From the moment that she'd heard Trish's voice on the other end of the line, she was compelled to come to the rescue.

Then Trish had been standing in front of her, makeup free with her hair flowing loose, wearing that robe. June wanted her, no matter what Trish said or did. Trish spoke so casually about seeing Katrina, acting like she had no idea how hurtful it was.

She told herself that this time she was really going to do it, she would cut Trish out of her life and never see her again. She'd come running over here like an idiot, and it couldn't happen again.

If June wasn't going to see her again, then what did it matter what happened right now, tonight? Trish had already rejected her in every way. June moved to touch her just to see what she would do, and she was half expecting to be pushed away. It took her breath away when Trish received her touch so eagerly, when it was clear how much Trish wanted her too.

Yet still she was ashamed, not so much that it had happened but because of her own lack of composure. You were supposed to lose control during sex, that was part of the fun of it, but she hated that Trish had seen her like that. June had not held a single piece of herself back.

June didn't need to be in love with someone before she had sex with them, but when she gave herself like that to someone she needed to believe that they at least respected her. Now she had been with a person who didn't care about her or her feelings one bit. The list was proof of what had been right in front of her all along.

When June finally got into her own bed, she began to sob. The tears poured out of her, her body heaving with them. She couldn't remember the last time that she'd cried, let alone like this.

Ollie said that she needed to go on a cleanse from Trish, and she had to admit that she had just done the opposite. June had binged, and now she would have to pay the price.

She could never see Trish again. She lay on her side, fists curled up, and cried herself into an exhausted sleep.

The alarm sounded, and Trish rolled over, picking up her phone and silencing it. She looked around the room and realized that June must have left some time after she had gone to sleep, which couldn't have been very long ago. Trish sat up, wiping her bleary eyes. She called out even though she was sure nobody would answer, sitting up in her bed and pulling the sheet around herself.

Trish went to her closet and pulled out a shirt, and then walked around the house. Her clothes were strewn across the floor in the living room, and her robe was in the hall. She started picking up her things. Of course, June's clothes were gone.

June hadn't left her a note. Trish couldn't figure out what her absence meant. June was always busy, but it was still early.

After everything that had passed between them, it was strange that she hadn't tried to wake Trish to say goodbye.

Although she hadn't slept much, Trish still wanted to go into work. It was rare for her to take sick days unless she was very unwell.

All morning at the library she looked for June. Trish stared at the entrance every time another student walked through the door, but June never came in. June must be tired and was most likely at home in bed. She'd had even less sleep than Trish, because she had come over straight from work at the bar.

When Trish was alone at the desk, it all came flooding to her. It had happened so fast, and it was so raw and urgent between them. Trish had never been uninhibited like that. It was strange and wonderful that she'd been that way, given that it was their first time. Even though Trish and June had not spoken much over recent weeks, she had trusted June enough to let herself go in a way that she never had with anyone else, not even Katrina.

During her lunch break, Trish sat in the breakroom and blew at the top of her mug to cool down her coffee. There was no way she could see Katrina again tonight. She picked up her phone and typed a message.

"I can't do tonight, we'll need to reschedule. I'll call you later."

"Hey, there," Trish said, turning her phone over as Ms. Rose pulled a chair up to the opposite side of the table.

"How was your weekend, dear?"

"Nothing special. How about you?"

"Very busy. Went to a leather bar, checked out a strip club on King Street. The usual."

Trish laughed, then covered her mouth as she yawned.

"You look tired. Late night?"

"Yes, but not because of anything as fun as a leather bar. My house was broken into last night."

"What are you even doing here today!" Ms. Rose said. "Why don't you take some sick leave and go home?"

"Thank you but I'm okay."

"It's quiet, we can manage without you. Go on home," Ms. Rose said, patting her arm.

Trish smiled at her. "You know, you're right, I should do that."

Trish used the free time when she arrived home to call a locksmith. It was a pointless exercise to have the locks changed but it made her feel better to do it. Once everything had been arranged, Trish sat and looked at her phone.

She had to call June. It wasn't right that they hadn't spoken since falling asleep in one another's arms. June had held her from behind, a hand splayed over her stomach while her face was buried in Trish's hair. June's breath was light on her skin. Right before she'd fallen asleep, June had kissed her shoulder. Trish was desperate to know how they had gone from that to the empty space in her bed. Her mind kept filling the space with ideas, like maybe June had been in another accident on her way home. There might be something serious that had prevented her from coming to the library that morning.

Finally, Trish drew a deep breath and dialed. As she had feared it might, her call went through to message bank, and she froze at the request to leave a message. Afterward she sat and stared at her screen for a long time.

Trish typed, "hello June" then changed it to "hey."

She deleted "Thank you for coming by," instead writing, "thank you so much for coming over."

"When can I see you?" was replaced by, "I hope I can see you soon."

She hit send, then sat staring at her phone to wait for a reply.

While she was still holding it, it rang, and Trish grimaced at Katrina's name on the screen.

"Hello," Katrina said, her tone clipped.

Trish's head dropped forward. "Hey Katrina, what's up?"

"I was wondering when you were going to call and explain why you broke our date."

"Someone broke into the house while I was sleeping last night," Trish mumbled.

"Someone broke in? You should have called me, I would have come over."

"Thanks, but I had someone else come around," Trish said.

"Oh. Leigh?"

"Not her, a friend."

"Well...I can come over now? We don't have to go out, but I could keep you company?" Katrina said.

"Thanks for offering, but I really just want to have an early night. I didn't get much sleep at all. I wouldn't be very good company anyway."

Trish imagined Katrina sitting on the other end of the line, trying to calculate how much further she could push things until Trish would relent. She was so good at wearing Trish down. Thankfully, she dropped it.

"How about the morning? I could get some coffee, buy a couple of things for breakfast. I'll cook. What do you think?"

Trish put a hand over her face. She wished she had the energy to just ask for more space. "Sure. That sounds great, thank you."

Trish got into bed after having checked the locks for the fifth time. She thought she would have trouble sleeping under the circumstances, but she was so weary that she fell asleep as soon as her head hit the pillow. She glanced at the clock when she woke up, shocked that it was almost time for Katrina to come over. Trish had told herself the night before that she was going to spend some time in the morning thinking about what she wanted to say to Katrina, and now there was no opportunity.

Katrina knocked at the door insistently until Trish answered. Coming inside, Katrina put down the coffee and the brown paper bag that held breakfast provisions, then hugged Trish. Trish stood stiffly, then brought her arms around Katrina.

"I'm so sorry. How did they get in? Were any of the windows broken?"

"Oh, they did something to pick the lock. I've already had them change it for a better one."

"Good, I'm glad to hear it. You let me know if there's anything I can do."

Katrina had released her, but her hand was on Trish's arm. Trish stared at the brown bag, not really seeing it.

"Shall I start getting this together?" Katrina asked.

Trish watched Katrina while she moved around the kitchen, cracking eggs into a pan and making toast. It struck Trish that especially toward the end of their relationship, they hadn't done much of this sort of thing. They never just hung out and talked. It was rare for her to have the feeling she had right now, that Katrina was looking after her. It made her wonder again whether Katrina had changed or if she was just on her best behavior.

Trish was studying her, looking for clues that might solve that mystery, when Katrina caught her eye.

"What are you thinking about?" Katrina asked.

"Nothing."

Asking Katrina how much of this was real wouldn't solve anything, it would just start a conversation that she wasn't ready to have.

Katrina served up breakfast, a heaped plate of scrambled eggs and bacon, which they ate out on the porch.

Trish looked down at her drive, wondering if June had parked there the night of the break-in or if she'd been out on the street.

It was one of winter's rare sunny days, the air crisp. It would be a great day to go for a motorbike ride. Maybe June was out riding right now. Trish wished they were together, so that she could feel the wind against her skin, her skin against June, and the solid plane of June's back against her.

"Penny for your thoughts?" Katrina said.

Trish shrugged. "Why do you keep asking me what I'm thinking? It's getting a bit much."

Katrina frowned. "Because of the way that you're behaving. All skitterish. Are you nervous about the break-in, is that it? I know it must have been pretty scary."

"Yes, it was," Trish said. "Very scary; it's freaked me out."

"Who was it that you had come over here, anyway?"

"I told you, a friend."

"I know that, I was just wondering which friend you're talking about?"

"You don't know her."

"Is it the same friend you went to watch play roller derby?"

"Yes," Trish said, examining her fingernails.

"So…who is she? How did you meet? Did you say she works at the university?"

"That is what I said, I met her through work. You know, you really are asking a lot of questions."

Katrina's knife and fork clattered to her plate. "Well, this 'friend' of yours is obviously someone you're close to, if you can call her in the middle of the night in an emergency. I'd really like to know who she is."

Katrina made sarcastic air quotes around the word "friend." Now she understood why Katrina had been so desperate to come over this morning. She was always more interested in something if someone else wanted it.

"What business is it of yours?" Trish said.

Trish couldn't seem to contain her anger today, and she wasn't sure if she even wanted to. She had never properly figured out whether she wanted Katrina back in her life and yet here she was, crowding her and taking up her morning.

All Trish wanted was to be by herself. That was her answer. It came to her so quickly that she couldn't understand why she had been ignoring the voice inside of her, over and over. It was obvious even before June had come over that she needed to end this.

"I think you're being really unfair now. If you didn't want me to come over, you should have said so."

Trish looked down into her coffee. It was true. She kept acting like all of this stuff with Katrina was something that was happening to her, instead of something that she was participating in. She was being as passive as she had always been with Katrina, and it was leaving her just as unhappy as she'd always been.

"All I'm asking for is for you to be honest with me. It's obvious that there's someone else in your life, I can see that things are different for you. Haven't I always been honest with you?" Katrina asked.

Trish had no intention of telling her anything. Her time with June was private, and she didn't want to cheapen it by arguing with Katrina about it.

"While we're asking questions, I actually have one for you," Trish said.

"Nice deflection!" Katrina said.

"Did your girlfriend really break up with you or was it the other way around?"

"What does that have to do with anything?"

"I think it's very relevant. You say that you're honest but you're not. You told me that you chose to break up with her. Look me in the eye and tell me that's really the case, and I'll be happy to drop it."

Katrina looked into her face and Trish felt nothing.

"It was a mutual decision."

"I don't think so. I think she dumped you, and you came back to me because you panicked."

"Where are you getting all this from? Trish, honey, you're wrong."

"I don't think I am. And you know what, I don't care if I am or not. This is a waste of both of our time. I think the right thing happened in the first place, and we should just both move on."

Trish stood up to clear her plate, and picked up Katrina's as well. She took no pleasure in Katrina's pain, yet now that they were out of her mouth she believed in the absolute truth of her words. That was more important than the way either of them might feel right now.

Trish walked to the kitchen and put the plates on the sink, leaning against the counter and taking a deep breath. She jumped when Katrina talked from behind her. "You've really made up your mind now, haven't you?"

Trish turned, her arms crossed over her chest.

"I could tell from the first time I came over here that you didn't love me anymore, you know," Katrina said. "I don't know why I persisted. I was hoping you'd remember how you'd felt before, and change your mind."

"Don't talk like that. I'm sorry this hasn't turned out the way you wanted, but I think we both know it's for the best if we don't see one another anymore. I'm sorry I didn't say this before today."

Katrina looked back at her, then went and picked up her handbag from the entry table.

"I wish you all the best," Trish said. She knew that she was risking that the words might sound trite, but she meant them, and she hoped that Katrina would understand that.

After a while, Katrina nodded back. "Same to you."

Katrina left, closing the door softly behind her. Trish sat down heavily on an armchair. It had all happened so quickly that it was making her head spin. She got up and went to find her folder, the one that held the lists of pros and cons. Trish pulled the papers from their folder and shook her head while she looked them over. How could she have ever thought something like this would be helpful?

Throwing them in the trash was not enough. Trish tore the pages into a hundred little pieces each. She would have burned them if she had a fireplace.

CHAPTER SEVENTEEN

June rifled through her papers. There was a page that had a quote highlighted on it, one that she wanted to use under a chapter title to introduce the subject. On her first pass, she couldn't find it, and she was making a mess. She stood up to clear a couple of dirty mugs from the table, then made separate piles of paper so that she could figure out what she'd already looked at. She was carefully reading over the pages again when a loud belt of laughter rang out from the living room.

For the past hour, she had been trying to ignore the voices coming from the next room. Max and Ollie were enjoying a morning of drinking coffee and talking while they watched Prince music videos online. Every now and then there was a loud noise, a phrase or laugh that broke through her concentration and grated on her nerves.

June settled back into work, and then Max's voice was raised as part of what sounded like a mock argument. She put her head in her hands.

This was why she started going to the university library so much in the first place. Since her decision to not go back there she'd been visiting a public library, but it was further away and it meant she wasted a lot of time getting to school for class. This morning she didn't have much time and just wanted to cram in as much work as she could. It was impossible with all this noise.

Ollie came into the kitchen and pulled a pizza box out of the fridge. He did it quietly, practically tip-toeing across the room, and that irritated her even more.

"I'm only going to be working in here for an hour or so, do you think you could keep it down until then?" June said.

"Sure."

"Thanks."

"You're welcome. What is going on with you?"

"Nothing. Sorry."

A chair scraped against the ground as Ollie pulled it out from the table and sat down. "Why are you here, anyway? You haven't worked from home in a long time."

"No reason, I just felt like it this morning. I've got an earlier class than usual. Covering for someone else."

"That doesn't make any sense when the library is on campus. That's why you go there, isn't it? What's happened with Trish? Did the cold turkey thing get too hard?"

June faced Ollie and looked him in the eye, because she knew she wouldn't get away with it otherwise. "Nothing. Like I told you, I just felt like it this morning."

Ollie looked back at her with narrowed eyes, and slowly got up from his seat and picked up the pizza box. "I'm here any time you want to tell me what's really going on."

Everywhere she looked, there were only empty spaces where June should be. Trish glanced at unoccupied desks as she passed them, almost able to see June sitting there with her work spread out before her. There was the cheeky grin, the thoughtful sigh, the slope of her neck as she put her hand there.

Trish had tried to call June four times now and each time it went through to voice mail. She was trying to accept the fact that June didn't want to hear from her, though at first she'd clung to the fantasy that there might be a good reason for it. Several times a day Trish started drafting a text message to June. The words were always inadequate, and they would go unanswered no matter what she said anyway.

When June was still coming to the library but basically ignoring her, it was painful, but not like this. At least she had the pleasure of looking at June. There were smiles now and then, or significant glances that she could tuck away. Those were the little things that convinced her there was still a connection between them, one that might be rekindled one day.

Now, she was just gone.

Trish went to the break room to make a pot of coffee. Each morning she dragged herself out of bed to go for a run, but she no longer enjoyed pushing herself. She was spending more time than ever by herself, filling her time with reading or anything that would disconnect her from her lonely reality.

It was too hard to be around Leigh and Andrew, because Trish still hadn't told her sister most of what had gone on with June. Leigh didn't even know about the failed attempt at dating Katrina again. Trish wanted to talk about it all, needed to, but she had no idea where to start. She was afraid that if she talked to Leigh it would really hit home how stupid she'd been, trying to juggle two women and ending up alone.

"Is there enough for me to have one as well?"

"Huh? Oh sure," Trish replied. She smiled vaguely at Ms. Rose, who kept having to remind her that she could call her Jodie.

They poured coffee into their mugs, and Trish went to take hers back to out to the main area of the library.

"Wait, why don't we sit for a minute? It's quiet, we don't need to get back out there right now."

"Sure," Trish said.

They had been sitting for a few moments when Jodie leaned forward, putting a hand on the table in front of her.

"I've been wanting to ask you something, Trish. Would you mind?"

"Of course not."

"Is there something wrong?"

"What do you mean? I haven't been messing up with anything, have I? I thought I was doing okay?"

Trish jumped when Jodie placed a hand on her own, patting it gently before she took it away. Trish's throat tightened at the compassion in Jodie's face. She hadn't been feeling very good about herself lately, or very likable.

"You've been doing as good a job as always. We don't know one another all that well but you just seem distracted to me, not quite yourself."

"I'm sorry."

"Nothing to apologize for, dear. I'm not asking you to make you feel self-conscious. But if you want to talk about anything, you can talk to me."

Trish's heart was beating hard, like she was an animal caught in a trap. Keeping her mask on and trying to be okay was wearing thin, and it didn't take much to crack it.

Jodie waited patiently while Trish gathered her thoughts.

"Actually, there have been some things going on. There was a woman that I was interested in, and things went bad. It was all my fault."

They both looked over their shoulders as one of the assistants came in. Trish's fingers toyed with the rim of her mug until he was gone.

"You mean the girl with the dark hair, who used to come in here a lot? The one who I saw you with at the café that time?"

Trish cleared her throat, unsure whether to confirm or deny it.

"Don't be embarrassed, it's just that…well it was always evident that there was something going on there. Between the two of you."

"Were we that obvious?" Trish replied. She wondered who else had noticed it.

"Only to those of us who know what to look for. I saw the way you two looked at each other and then when I saw you at the café, I did wonder if you were together."

"Her name's June. She's a writer."

"That's right, I'd forgotten her name. Anne told me. So, what happened between you and June? Did you break up?"

Trish shifted in her chair. There were so many things about their story that she would never want to tell Jodie. "I don't know, we weren't ever together. It's hard to explain. It's all just a little bit complicated."

"Complicated? That's what the kids are calling it nowadays, I know. In my experience, things are only as complicated as you make them. If you did something wrong, apologize, and if she did something wrong, forgive her. Work through it."

"I appreciate the advice but unfortunately I don't think things can always be fixed with an apology. Not when you've acted like I have."

Jodie nodded, but Trish could see that she wasn't convinced. "They can't always, but if you've done something wrong you should apologize, whether you think you'll be forgiven or not. If it's the right thing you should do it, and then as a bonus you can have a clear conscience," Jodie said.

"You have strong opinions on this sort of stuff, huh?"

"I didn't get this far in life without learning a few things. I especially haven't lasted in a relationship for twenty-five years without knowing what I'm doing. Trust me, an apology costs you nothing and it can never do any harm."

"Well, thank you. It means a lot that you care enough to try and help me," Trish said.

Jodie nodded, satisfied that she had gotten her point across.

Trish returned to her work, Jodie's words drifting across her mind throughout the afternoon. The relationship that she'd built with June had always been ambiguous, transforming from friendship into something more and then back again. The whole time, June had done nothing but go with the flow, though only a fool would think that June was okay with all that had happened.

It was clear that by the end, Trish's behavior was hurting her. Yet it had never occurred to Trish to apologize properly, and now she wondered why that was. It had just always been easier to bury her head in the sand and hope that things would work out, exactly like she'd done her entire life. It was too scary to tell June how she felt, to talk about what she'd been doing.

If she was honest, she could admit that she always thought that June would let her get away with things. June was so easygoing and tolerant; it was as though nothing ever bothered her. Or was that just a convenient way of seeing things?

It hit her all at once, how right Jodie was. Trish couldn't bear the thought of never seeing June again, but she especially could not bear the thought of never getting the chance to right the wrongs that she had committed. She needed desperately for June to know how sorry she was, for everything.

* * *

June and Ollie sat side by side on the sofa, watching *Married At First Sight.* They both claimed to hate reality TV, but they always watched whenever they had the chance.

Ollie was screaming with laughter at the scene of a couple fighting, the camera following them around a room as they yelled at one another. It was cut together with talking head shots of the woman explaining why her new husband wasn't meeting her needs. "You just could not make this shit up. Did you hear what she just said?"

"It's all fake anyway, you're so gullible," June said, her arms crossed across her chest. Usually she would be laughing right along with him, but tonight the tone of the show was hitting her the wrong way. It felt mean-spirited.

Ollie didn't reply. She glanced over at him to see that he was now looking at the screen and frowning.

"I'm sorry, I know I'm being a drag."

He shrugged. "It's okay."

They sat watching the rest of the show in silence.

It was nearly two weeks since she'd had spent the night with Trish, and it wasn't getting any easier. Trish still occupied way too much real estate in June's mind. She couldn't deal with the free-floating dread about the whole situation. Whenever she took a moment to step back and examine what was going on underneath that feeling, she realized she was terrified she might never see Trish again.

It was what she needed to do, though. She ignored Trish's calls, burning with resentment about how much she wanted to answer them. The ringing phone was torture, and so was seeing Trish's name on the screen. June fought the urge to text Trish and tell her to go away. It would only ruin the clean break she was trying to achieve.

When the show finished, Ollie got up to go to the kitchen. June had a strange sensation when he left, that she'd been abandoned. She had been discovering these past couple of weeks how much her need for privacy was costing her. Not telling Ollie so that she wouldn't risk his judgement of her also meant that there was nobody to comfort her. She had never felt so alone.

With that thought came sudden tears, a torrent that she didn't even know she had been holding back. She balled her fists while tears rolled quietly down her face, her throat aching. When Ollie came back into the room she didn't notice, and covered her face too late. She couldn't look at him, holding a hand over her eyes while she stared down at the floor. It occurred to her that this was the second time she had cried over Trish recently, and it was more than she had cried in the last five years put together.

The warm weight of Ollie's arm fell around her shoulders and she leaned into him. He held her while she burrowed her face into his shirt and cried. It took a while for her to be done, but at last the end came.

She wiped her face with her shirt, getting her breath back.

"Honey, I don't know what to say," Ollie said. "I've never even seen you cry before. It's kind of scary. If you won't tell me what's wrong, I don't know what I can do."

June leaned back on the seat and took a deep breath. "It's about Trish."

"Okay," he said.

"We slept together. I went over to her house one night, and it happened then, even though she was making me feel like shit again. I just really miss her. I know I've been so stupid. You must think I'm really stupid."

"I don't think you're stupid at all," he said softly. "You really love her, don't you?"

"No," she said. "I don't."

He tilted his head and looked at her, his face open and uncritical. "June."

"I have strong feelings for her, I guess."

"Okay. Put it however you like, but I've never known you to act like this before. She's gotten under your skin."

"So, what do I do now? How can I feel better?"

"I wish I could tell you. You need to do whatever you need to do to get through this. Whatever you think is right."

June sighed. "I know I can't see her anymore. It will get better over time, I just need to be patient."

They sat together, June burrowing her head into his shoulder.

* * *

June paced back and forth in front of her students, gesturing as she spoke. The only time she felt good lately was when she was teaching a class. Working at the bar could be exhausting but there were always lulls, quiet times in which she had too much space to think. Even the apathy of her students couldn't change the fact that she felt useful in front of the classroom, fully engaged with it whether they were listening to her or she was working hard to get their attention.

When she was teaching, she could see a future for herself, one in which she wasn't so sad all the time. One in which she wasn't labelling herself with some of the things Trish had written on her list. She couldn't believe Trish thought she was unstable, or that she had a problem with June not having a steady enough job. The words stung every time they came into her mind.

June checked the clock and saw that she had run a few minutes over time. She was on a roll about novels that spoke to the immigrant experience in Australia, and it was surprising that none of her students had interrupted her to tell her.

"Sorry guys, I've cut into your break," she said. "So, think about what I've just said, and I'd love to hear your reflections on it next class."

June watched with satisfaction as the students packed up their notebooks and pens.

The good cry she'd had the night before left her a sense of peace. Her eyes were sore and tired but she'd needed to break a little, to stop bottling things up so much.

"Thanks, miss," Jacob said as he exited.

June smiled. She wasn't much older than a lot of her students, but to people like Jacob eight years or so made her ancient. June watched him go out into the hall. There was someone standing just outside of the classroom, watching her.

June's fists balled up and loosened again.

How could Trish come here? This was one of the places that she counted on for privacy, depending on it for her worlds to remain separate. She looked down at her desk, putting her hand on it and staring at it where it lay. The last students left the room, packing up their things and chatting, and then it was quiet. Only then did she dare to look up again. Trish was still there, standing outside and looking in the window at her.

June met her eye, then pointedly looked away, turning to clean the whiteboard behind her with angry strokes. Maybe by the time she was done, Trish would finally get the message and leave.

She jumped when Trish's voice came, close behind her. "June. I need to talk to you."

CHAPTER EIGHTEEN

It was not as though she could ever forget what Trish looked like, but the force of her physical presence still took June's breath away. There were dark circles around her eyes and her face was gaunt, but still she was the most beautiful woman June had ever seen. It was exactly why June needed her to stay away.

At last, June found the strength to meet her eye. Trish's expression stabbed through her. It was full of sadness, and June had the maddening impulse to hug her. Instead, June pulled her arms across her chest.

"What are you doing here, Trish?"

"I'm sorry. I know you're working. I know I shouldn't be here. I just…I didn't know what else to do," Trish said, her voice wavering. "Where did you go?"

June shrugged. She needed to get through these few minutes, to harden herself enough to be able to walk away. Then she would be on her own again, and she could try to forget this desperate feeling.

"It looked like your students were really into your class. You're a good teacher, but then I always knew you would be."

June didn't react, though the words gave her an unwanted sense of pride. It was pathetic that she still wanted Trish's approval.

"Are you doing anything now? I'm on my break so I don't have much time, but I was wondering if you might come for a walk with me, so that we can talk?" Trish asked.

June shook her head, shrugging again.

"Can I please have the chance to explain things? I need to apologize to you. Even if it doesn't change anything, I think it's important. For both of us."

"Don't try and tell me what's important for me. I don't think you'd even know what you were apologizing for," June muttered, moving to walk past Trish.

Trish put a hand on June's arm, lightly encircling it with her fingers. "Please, June. Just a few minutes of your time. Then you never have to see me again. I won't come back again, I promise."

They were staring at one another now. June let out a nervous laugh. She didn't know whether she wanted to push Trish or kiss her, and it was terrifying.

"Get your hand off me right now. I didn't say you could touch me."

Trish's touch dropped away. "Sorry. Please know that I care about you. I've made a lot of mistakes, and you didn't deserve to be on the receiving end of all of it, all my confusion. I wish I could take it all back. I'd do anything for a fresh start."

"It's too late. I could never forget the way you've treated me."

"I deserve that, one hundred percent. But don't you think that what we have is worth fighting for? I think so."

"And what is it exactly that you think we have?"

Trish moved closer to her, not touching her with anything other than her steady gaze, following June's eyes as she tried to avert them. Trish's shampoo smell was clean and sweet, familiar from when they'd been lying together. She remembered the last time they'd argued like this, and it was all she could do to not push into Trish again, to sink into her and soothe this aching need.

"Something special. I know how mad you are at me right now, and you have every right to be, but maybe one day in the future things could be better between us. If you can find it in your heart to forgive me."

"That's interesting. Don't you worry that I don't have enough stability? Seeing as I'm…what was it you wrote? Not a serious person? I mean, if we hang out, wouldn't that mean you might have to hang out with my horrible friends?" June said.

"How did you…" Trish took a step back, her eyes wide.

"It was on the table, I knocked it off when I was leaving. I saw it all."

Trish looked back at her, openmouthed.

"Don't worry about it, I already knew that you felt that way. It wasn't any big shock, considering the way you treated me. Still a strange thing to do, though, don't you think? How would you like it if I wrote a list of everything I don't like about you? How about the fact that you're materialistic? That you have a great big stick up your ass? You're too judgmental, how about that one?"

Trish had tears standing in her eyes. June shook her head and looked away so that she wouldn't have to see them. "I didn't mean to say all that. Forget about it. Just leave me alone, okay?"

"I'm so sorry June," Trish said, her voice small.

June pushed past her, out into the hall, and walked down the stairs as quickly as her legs would carry her.

Trish returned to work with her stomach churning. It never occurred to her that June might have seen those stupid lists. She wanted to go home and look at them, to remind herself exactly what they said, but then she remembered she destroyed them. Trish wished desperately that she'd destroyed them sooner, or never written them at all.

She put her hand on her stomach. It was over for them, June couldn't have made that clearer, but it didn't feel over to her. Trish couldn't bear that June would always remember her as the person who'd written those things about her.

Now June believed that Trish had added her up like a sum, and came out with the wrong answer. Writing the list had been so stupid, and she'd only done it because she had never been able to trust her own feelings. How could she convey to June how meaningless it had been to her?

There was no coming back from this.

"Good lord what's wrong with you, are you sick?" Jodie asked. She put a hand to Trish's forehead. "You look terrible."

Trish tried to laugh. "I'm fine, just feeling a bit queasy."

"Do you need to go home?"

"You know what, I really should. I could do with a good lie down, I think."

"Look after yourself," Jodie said, and it sounded like an order. Trish could tell by the way Jodie was looking at her that she wanted to ask more questions, but thankfully she let Trish go without another word.

Trish went directly to Leigh's place, unable to bear the thought of being by herself all afternoon.

"Trish! What are you doing here?" Leigh said when she opened the door.

"I think I might have put on some weight. Do you mind if I try the dress on again, just to reassure myself?"

Leigh looked her up and down. "Okay, but I think you're being silly, you don't look like you've put on any weight to me."

"Can I just try it on, please?"

Leigh crossed her arms and frowned. "What gives? Aren't you supposed to be at work?"

"No, I finished early. I thought you'd be happy about this, we don't want to leave it 'til the last minute and find out it has to be altered, right?"

"Riiiiight," Leigh said. "Go then, it's in the spare room."

Trish took the dress out of its garment bag. Leigh said that she wanted her bridesmaids to have something they'd want to wear again; it was a strapless burgundy gown that flared out at the hips. Trish slid the zip up her back. She wished she'd thought of a better reason for coming over out of the blue, because she really wasn't in the mood for this.

Leigh knocked on the door. Without waiting for an answer, she pushed her way into the room.

"See I told you that you were being silly, if anything you've lost weight!"

Trish looked back at her helplessly, and burst into tears.

"Come on, get out of that thing and come out to the kitchen, I'll make us some tea or something," Leigh said.

Trish cried as she stepped out of the dress, and was still crying when she explained what had happened with June. They stood at the kitchen counter, cradling cups of tea while Trish talked.

"You and your damn lists!" Leigh said, handing her a tissue. "You don't know when to stop."

Trish raised her eyebrows and pointed to a list on the fridge.

"That's different, I'm getting married. I have a lot to organize right now. It would be impossible for me to keep track without them."

"I know, but I'm begging you, can we please stop talking about the list? You're starting to make me wish I hadn't told you. I already feel bad enough."

"Sorry. But that's really the icing on the cake in this whole thing. I bet it wouldn't be so bad if she hadn't seen that. She might have been able to get over the other stuff. Well, then there's the Katrina thing. I can't believe you weren't more thoughtful about all that. How would you feel if she were dating someone else, flaunting it like that and telling you all about it?"

Trish threw her head back, somewhere between crying and laughing. "Leigh! Can you stop rubbing salt in my wounds? I came here for support, not to be told how stupid I've been. I already know that."

"You should have kept me updated, I could have really helped you avoid some of your bigger mistakes. I would have told you June was only doing that silly romantic friendship thing because she wanted to get close to you. I've never heard of anything so dumb. You should have seen right through that. And like, the whole Katrina issue, I can't believe you even considered it. Ugh."

"Honestly? Neither can I. It was all very unpleasant. I didn't consider it, not really. I should never have gone there, though."

"Damn right you shouldn't. June's so cool, and nice. Katrina's not fit to lick her boots, to tell you the truth."

"I really like her," Trish said helplessly.

Leigh handed Trish another cookie. "I can't believe you made me break my wedding shredding diet for this."

"You opened them! I didn't ask you to," Trish said.

"Whatever. So, what's your next move?"

Trish stuffed the cookie in her mouth. "There's no next move. She couldn't have been any clearer. I'm just going to have to get over it."

"You're kidding. You can't leave it like that!"

"Stalking is illegal in this state last time I checked. I was already pushing it going to see her at work."

Leigh sighed. "Oh, Trish, you've always been such a quitter. Always taking the path of least resistance."

"What exactly do you propose I do?"

"Make a grand gesture. She's already mad at you, what's the worst that can happen if you give it one last shot?"

"A grand gesture? Like what?"

"I don't know what she'd like, I don't know her as well as you do. It needs to be something personal. Something just between the two of you. You'll know the right thing to do if you give it some thought."

That night Trish lay on her sofa, thinking about every romance movie she had ever watched, and ran through every make-up scene in fiction that she could think of. She considered special songs and performances, expensive dates and gifts, and yelling for June outside of her window with a stereo over her head. Everything that crossed her mind was ridiculous, and she couldn't imagine June going for any of it.

It had to be something that Trish would have time to deliver before June could cut her off. That added an extra layer of difficulty.

There was so much she wished she could say to June. Yet, she'd never been all that good with words, and when it came to June, all she had ever done was put her foot in her mouth. If only she could be eloquent, if only she was the sort of person who could find the right words to capture everything.

It had to be a letter. As soon as she thought of it, she knew it was right. It wasn't exactly a grand gesture, but it would be sincere, and it would mean she was being true to who she was. Writing to June would give her time to digest Trish's words. There could be no more ambushes, like what she had done when she'd gone to June's classroom. Even if June made the decision to not forgive her, there was something comforting to Trish about the idea of spilling it all onto the page.

Trish jumped up from the sofa, arranging herself at the table with a notepad and pen.

It took her hours, because she approached the letter in her usual methodical fashion. Though she had always wanted to write, she didn't consider herself a natural author. She didn't have any special skill in transforming her words into sentences and paragraphs, especially not when it came to emotions. It was something that she had to plan, no matter how much the sentiment was from her heart.

Trish began by writing bullet points that set out exactly what she wanted to communicate. It was important that she explain herself and tell June why she had been acting the way she had, but the worst thing she could do was write something that was all about herself. She wanted to focus not just on the way that June made her feel, but on why June was everything that she wanted in another person. And she had to do it in a way that would blot out the memory of those damaging lists and everything they said.

Trish drafted and redrafted, reading the words aloud to herself each time to see if they were working. When it was right, she would know. When she was finished, she went to bed and slept on it, and then when she got out of bed just after dawn she rewrote it one more time.

At last she was satisfied. Trish crisply folded the letter and sealed it in an envelope. She was going to mail it, because she didn't want to risk being discovered if she tried to slip it into June's mailbox.

Dear June,

I know that I owe you an explanation, but that you don't owe it to me to hear it. Still, I hope that you'll keep reading.

Once there was a time when I would have said, "if you care about someone enough then fear doesn't matter." I would have said that fear could never be a reasonable excuse for treating someone the way that I've treated you (and I'd be right, wouldn't I?). I would have said that there must be some other reason someone would act this way, because if you hide behind fear then you just don't care enough. I feel differently now. I still believe that it's not a reasonable excuse, but I do care about you, and still I let fear get in the way. I'll always regret that.

I don't know what happened to the person that scoffed at the idea that fear could make a person act the way that I have acted. The simple answer is that I've gotten older and somehow not at all wiser. My experiences have not made me brave as you should be brave when you've lost something, especially if you ever hope to be happy again.

I was with a person for a long time that taught me a lot of bad habits. I learned to mistrust myself, and to think that my feelings don't mean much. I don't blame Katrina and I know that I played my part in all of it. One day, if you let me, I'll tell you about all the ways that she's your opposite. I'll tell you how you've allowed me to imagine a different way of being with someone. You make me feel good about myself and I wish that you could say the same about me.

You know that I'm a rule follower. Rules are necessary, but I've always overestimated how important they are. I'm trying to face the fact that I grab on to them because I don't know who I am sometimes. Katrina is supposed to be the type of person that I should be with for no other reason than that she follows the same set of rules that I do.

You might be wondering what it is about you that makes you someone that goes against these all-important rules. You saw my stupid list, you know what I've thought. But you think it's a judgment against you, when it's myself that I doubt. We come from different worlds. I've always wondered what you would see in me, someone who is older, conventional, and dull. I'm a librarian! I would never dream of strapping on a pair of skates, or riding a motor bike, or working two jobs so that I could pursue my dreams.

That is why you scare me, because I was always sure that if we were ever to be together I would bore you and it would be over almost before it had begun. If I've ever made you feel like I thought you're not good enough it's just my own stupid projection. I've worried that I'm not good enough for you, and that if you didn't already know that then you would figure it out soon enough.

The reasons that you are against the rules are the exact same things that attract me. Seeing as I'm so good at making lists (!) I will tell you some of the things that I love about you. I love your wit, your toughness, your beauty, and intelligence. I love your drive, your talent, and your sense of fun. I love the million things that make up who you are that I can't define.

I wish I could rewind to when I met you. I'd relive every interaction with you, but I'd do everything differently. Instead of trying to run away from you all the time, I would run toward you.

We could never have been friends and it was foolish to try. I take full responsibility for everything. Trying to be your friend is one of the biggest mistakes I've made. I just didn't know how to do it. I wanted to be near you, and I was so selfish. I should have been brave enough to date you when you asked me, and I'll regret it forever that I didn't have the courage.

You were right about romantic friendships, they can't exist like that, at least not for people like you and me.

I hope that there are some good times that you can remember about us. I know that I will always remember them, and I'll always remember you.

You know where I am if you ever want to talk to me. I'd give anything to talk to you.

Love, Trish.

CHAPTER NINETEEN

Each day Trish slid her fingers cautiously into her mailbox, wondering when she would find the letter returned and unopened. The fact that it wasn't there brought her a relief that never lasted for long. June could just as easily have thrown her letter away.

Trish promised herself that if two weeks passed and there was no response, she would accept that there was never going to be one. At some point, she had to move on, and she would have to take some small comfort in knowing that at least she had given it one last try.

The two weeks dragged by, the days long and dreary. Trish fantasized about having one last chance to rewrite that letter. It scrolled through her head constantly, and she fixated on sentences that could be misinterpreted. Still, she decided that she wouldn't mind if June were to come storming into the library to throw the torn-up letter in her face. At least it would be something.

Trish survived each evening by distracting herself. She thoroughly cleaned the house, and while she worked she planned what she was going to do next. When this wait was over, she would try making new friends. She could invite Jodie over to dinner, because that was a friendship that she wanted to cultivate. They'd been talking a lot at work and now that things were out in the open, they'd really been hitting it off. It might help to join some type of class or group, something on her own without Leigh so that she would be forced to put herself out there. This loneliness was not something that she was willing to live with for long.

The two-week deadline came, and there was nothing. On the night it passed, Trish went to bed with her stomach hollowed out, sick and sad. She cried like a child, lying stiff as a board on the mattress. The deadline was arbitrary, something that she had made up all on her own, but it felt like she had lost something all over again. It didn't matter how much she'd tried to keep her expectations low, she'd still believed that there was a chance. Now it was gone, and her hope seemed foolish. June had made her decision, and a stupid letter was never going to change it.

Trish had the next day off from work, something she'd organized because she wanted to take some time out for herself. Throughout the last two weeks of waiting she'd been taut as a bow string. Now she woke up sick of crying with sore eyes; she just couldn't do it anymore. She rolled out of bed, downing a glass of water that was on the nightstand.

She pulled on her leggings and a sweater to go jogging. When she got home, she cooked a pot of minestrone soup to take to work for lunch for the week. Afterward she paced around the house. She snatched up her copy of *Infinity*, deciding that she'd take it around to Gina's Place to read.

Trish brooded over her coffee. She'd done what she could to salvage things, but it was really over, and there was no choice but to move on. While she'd been spending time with June, she'd been a happier person. Not only was she going to miss June, she would miss the person she'd been with her.

It wasn't going to be easy, but she wanted to make herself be happy on her own.

Trish walked home, then sat out on the porch with her tablet, laying a list of ideas for what she could do down next to her. Aside from researching social groups and gyms she might want to join, she was going to work on finally getting herself a cat. It would be nice to have someone to talk to when she got home from work, and someone to care whether she was around or not.

There was the roar of an engine on the street but Trish kept her eyes trained on her tablet. For two weeks, she'd run to the window at the sound of every car. It had to stop.

The noise could only be ignored for so long. It was growing louder, and Trish's focus snapped up, following the familiar red and black bike as it pulled into her driveway.

Trish leapt from her seat. Even after all that waiting, she wasn't ready for this. If only she could pause this moment, because anything might happen in the next. For now, there was June sliding off the bike, pulling the helmet from her head. Trish put her hand tightly on the railing and met her gaze, trying to read June's purpose in it. What if June just wanted to have one final talk with her, to tell Trish again to leave her alone?

It was better than nothing.

Trish froze. It occurred to her that she could walk down the stairs and meet June, but it made more sense to talk inside the house. She didn't know if she should invite her up. She didn't know what to do at all.

June broke eye contact and disappeared out of view, and then Trish could hear the sounds made by her footsteps as she ascended the stairs.

They were face-to-face, and still Trish couldn't guess what June's intent was. Her expression was serious, and it didn't change when Trish tried to smile at her.

It was so overwhelming to look at her. Trish had thought that June's face was fixed well in her mind, but it always seemed like June was a little different than she remembered. Now she was even more stunning, though there was something fragile about the way she looked. There were dark circles under her eyes and again Trish suspected that like herself, June had not been getting enough sleep.

"I thought you weren't going to come," Trish said.

"I needed to think about a few things."

"And, what did you decide?" Trish said.

June put her hands together as though in prayer, placing them up against her face. "I'm not sure. I don't know. I thought I might know when I saw you."

She pulled her hands away from her face and laughed, until Trish was laughing along with her. The release soothed her, and for the first time in weeks the weight was lifted from her shoulders.

"Do you want to sit with me and talk?" Trish asked, forcing her hands to stay at her sides. She could clutch at June right now. She would do anything to keep her here.

"I think I might keep going, actually. But I've at least decided I'm going to start coming back to the library. Okay?"

"Okay," Trish agreed, a smile breaking out on her face.

It wasn't a promise, it wasn't much at all really, and Trish closed her mouth against asking more about what it meant. At least she would be able to see June all the time again. It meant that June might not hate her.

June smiled back at her. "I'll see you there, then."

She turned to go, and Trish watched her back as she walked away, throwing one quick glance over her shoulder as she walked down the stairs. Trish sat back down, unable to believe it. June had come.

Trish didn't have to wait long to see her again, though it felt like an age. The next day she watched June come into the library like she had so many times before, her backpack slung over her shoulder, sauntering in like she'd never been gone. She nodded toward Trish before she found her seat. The half smile she used to acknowledge Trish was a miracle.

Trish knew better than to go to her. Instead, she tried to just take pleasure in June's presence, glancing over at her every time she had an opportunity, to reassure herself that she was still there. Whenever she caught June looking back at her, heat gathered between her legs. It was even stronger than it had been before all of this had happened.

There was a powerful sense of déjà vu associated with all this. Trish wanted to believe that it meant that June was ready to be friends with her again, and with any luck much more than that. Yet how could she know when June had barely said a word to her? There was no way of knowing how long they'd play this game. Trish tried to put those thoughts out of her mind and just enjoy that they were in the same room together again.

Trish was organizing overdue notices when she sensed a presence at the counter, and she looked up to find June standing there, staring back at her.

"Hel-Hello," Trish said.

"Hey there," June said, sticking out her hand as well as her chin. "I'm June."

Trish blinked at June and took her hand to shake it, playing along even if she didn't quite get the joke. The fingers were warm in her hand. She didn't let them go for a long time. If she could, she would pick up that hand and press her lips to it. June nodded at Trish, silently urging her to do something.

"My name's Trish?" she said.

"Hello, Trish. You're the new librarian here, aren't you?"

"Yes," Trish said, then frowned. What was this exactly? She looked back at June, who was waiting for her to say more.

"I'm sorry, what are we doing?" Trish asked. "I don't get it."

June raised her eyebrows. "Really now? You can't figure it out? I thought it would be obvious."

"Well, you'll have to excuse me, but it's not obvious to me," Trish said. As soon as the words were out of her mouth, June's meaning started to register. "Hold up, is this us starting all over again?"

"You said that was what you wanted."

"Please. Begin at the beginning, I have it now. I can do it properly."

June was shaking her head at her, but she was laughing. "Okay. Now it's a third start. It's not really fresh anymore, but okay, we can do it again if you want."

"Come on then!" Trish said.

June held her hand out again and this time Trish clasped it for even longer before letting it go. Trish leaned over the counter, pushing her hair behind her ear.

"Hello, I'm June. You must be the new librarian here?"

"Yes, I am, my name's Trish. And what's your purpose here, June?"

"I'm actually not a student here, I use this library to work on a book I'm writing. And I'm a tutor at the university."

"You are? That's wonderful. It sounds to me like there would be no ethical conflicts here for me at all. And exactly how old are you, June?"

June tried to not smile and failed. "I'm twenty-six years old. How do you feel about younger women?"

"That's barely any younger than me at all. Why should age matter anyway?"

"Indeed," June agreed. "I don't see why it should."

"I would really love to take you out. What do you think about that?"

June looked down at the desk between them and when she looked up, her eyes were clear and calm. "I'd like that a lot."

They failed miserably in carrying out their plans of going on a date.

June had offered to pick Trish up on her bike. After riding over to Trish's house, she stood looking up at it, hoping that she hadn't made a mistake. Then she decided she didn't care if she had; her stomach was doing somersaults at the thought of being with Trish again.

June climbed the steps, enjoying the delicious anticipation of knowing that Trish would be waiting for her on the other side of the door. She'd dressed in black jeans and a patterned black-and-white button-up, and she unzipped her jacket so Trish could see it.

Trish opened the door, stunning in a green dress. June greeted Trish with a kiss on the cheek, standing close to her. Before she leaned in, Trish eyed her body admiringly. Then Trish moved to June's other cheek to kiss her too.

June felt the soft brush of her lips, and Trish's hand lightly but confidently gripping her elbow. The smell of Trish's hair came to her, so lovely. June put a hand on Trish's shoulder and they stood in place for a moment together, breathing one another in. Finally, Trish turned her head and captured June's lips. The sweetness of them slid over June's mouth. Trish gripped her waist, making her weak.

After a few minutes of fevered making out in the doorway, Trish pulled June inside. She took June's wrist and walked them directly to her bedroom, then started to strip June efficiently, unbuttoning her shirt. June let it happen while she watched Trish's face, loving the expressions that passed over it. Trish splayed a hand across her stomach and June shivered as Trish's hands reached up to her breasts.

Trish slowly pushed June's shirt from her shoulders and June leaned in, kissing Trish again.

June walked them forward, feeling the jolt as the back of Trish's knees hit the bed. Trish guided them down onto the mattress and June climbed on top of her. The two of them kissed hard, and their ragged breathing filled the room.

June reached between them and slid her hand up and underneath Trish's dress, grabbing Trish's thigh as Trish's legs came around her waist. Trish sighed out her name, and June kissed her open mouth.

"I've really missed you," Trish whispered.

June kissed Trish's neck softly, then moved her mouth close to Trish's ear. "I missed you too."

June was going to show her exactly how much. She reached up higher, edging her fingers closer to where she wanted them to be, a hand slipping around to touch Trish's inner thigh. Trish sighed into her ear and June kissed her neck, Trish squirming deliciously underneath her.

June drew back and stood up, intending to take the rest of her clothes off, but she only got as far as her shoes and socks before Trish's mouth was on her again. Trish sat on the edge of the bed and grabbed her by the hips, kissing her stomach, reaching for the button of her jeans. June looked down at her upturned face, putting a palm to her cheek.

Wordlessly, June undressed, not taking her eyes from Trish as she did the same. Trish shyly unhooked her bra, working it down her arms and dropping it on the floor before stepping out of her underwear. June had seen Trish naked before, but she'd never felt like they had all this time, and now she drank in the sight. The curve of Trish's hips, her beautiful skin. Trish sat on the bed, looking back up at her. The sight of her stopped June's breath.

"I think you missed something. I mean, if you don't mind?" June said, gesturing to Trish's hair.

Trish smiled at her and loosened her hair from its ponytail. "You've got a thing about that, don't you?"

"It does seem that way."

"What are you still doing standing all the way over there?" Trish asked.

"Looking at you," June said. "You're so beautiful."

Trish closed her eyes, her chest rising and falling with deep breaths, and she then moved back on the bed to lie down. "Hurry up and come over here."

June followed where Trish had led her, then they lay face-to-face. Trish pulled her close to embrace her, and their skin was touching from their feet up to their foreheads. It almost felt like enough to just lie here like this. But then Trish kissed her, and she knew she needed more.

June rolled Trish underneath her, and ran the tips of her fingers down Trish's ribs and then her stomach, watching the sharp intake of breath. Trish put an arm around her neck and through her hair, and June leaned down toward her.

Their kisses were unhurried, and June had never experienced anything like the slow burn that built between them as they pressed themselves together.

June lazily brought her hand down to Trish's breast and gently ran her fingers over it, again and again while they kissed. Now and then she ran the back of her fingers over Trish's ribs and over her hip. Trish pulled her mouth away breathlessly.

"June, please," Trish said.

"What is it?"

"You're driving me crazy."

"Oh," June said.

She rose up and grabbed Trish's wrists, pinning them against the mattress, smiling back at Trish when she laughed. June held her while she bent and licked her way down Trish's neck, moving down to take a nipple in her mouth. Trish cried out, her back arching as June flicked her tongue against the peak. June released Trish's wrists now, too focused on her task for games. She flattened her tongue and ran it over Trish's breasts and down lower, feeling Trish suck in her stomach.

At last, June moved back up and laced her arm underneath Trish's shoulders and around her neck, cradling her. She reached her other hand down between them, her eyes on Trish's face as she drew it lower and lower. As her fingers found Trish ready for her, she saw the moment register in Trish's expression, full of pleasure and need. Their eyes were locked as June stroked her and their hips moved together, Trish's head falling back against her arm. Trish's eyes never left her own and June gazed down into them, trying to tell her with every movement of her hand and every kiss what this was to her.

Trish's hand was pressed against her back, and the other reached up to the side of June's face. Her leg was drawn up, bent at the knee as she pushed down into the bed, and she was biting her lip. June wanted to freeze the moment in her mind, sure that she'd never seen anything so gorgeous.

June was kissing her when Trish released a shuddering sigh into her mouth, a fist balling in her hair.

"June," Trish said softly, just that one word, but June knew what she meant.

Trish stretched, arching her back until the sheet started to slip down her body. June looked over her naked form, wanting to see her again, and then June laid her head upon Trish's shoulder. Trish's arms were wrapped around her, her fingers in June's hair.

"My letter must have been really good," Trish said.

June laughed against her chest. Trish sounded so proud of herself.

"Well?"

"It helped," June said.

"What do you mean, it helped? Wasn't it the whole thing? I didn't do anything else."

"I mean, I'd been trying to get over you, and the letter helped me realize it was never going to work. I was always going to be waiting for you to do something else, hoping you'd come to me again."

"I thought you didn't like it when I saw you at your class."

June shrugged, trailing her fingers over Trish's ribs. Even though she'd been furious at Trish for coming by that day, there was still a part of her that wanted her to try again.

"Did it clear everything up enough?" Trish moved, pulling out from under June and rolling onto her side so that they could see one another's eyes. June obliged, turning and facing her.

June's finger lifted and traced her jawline, then ran over her lips. "It did. It explained a lot of things."

"I know we're joking about having a fresh start and everything, but I guess I just want to know…"

"If it really is a fresh start?" June broke in.

Trish nodded. "Exactly. You have no idea how happy I am to be here with you. But I want to start this out right. I don't want us to start this thing but still have it hanging between us. I wouldn't blame you if you were still mad. If you are, I think now's the time to tell me. Let's get it all out there and work through it, otherwise things might go bad later. What do you think?"

"I don't think I could be here if I was still holding on to everything. When I saw you here the other day, I was pretty sure I was going to be okay, but I needed to go away and think some more after I'd seen you."

"I was wondering what was going through your head when you came over that day."

"It kind of knocked me down, seeing you again. So, I went away and searched myself, and I realized that I didn't feel angry anymore."

"So, you really do think you can forget about all of the stuff I did?"

June again put her fingers on Trish's face, smoothing the line of her brow. "Don't take this the wrong way, but how could I forget about it? I don't want to forget about anything that's happened since we met. If I forgot the stuff that caused me pain I wouldn't remember all the happiness I've had, too. Now that I know you're serious about this I wouldn't want anything to be any different."

Tears sprung to Trish's eyes. "Do you really mean that?"

"I don't say anything I don't mean. For example, you should kiss me now."

That night they drove to get takeout from a Chinese restaurant, then they took the brown paper bag of honey chicken, rice, and egg rolls to St Kilda beach. It was nearing the end of winter, the air still cool on their skin. They brought a checked woolen blanket from the car down to the sand, draping it over their shoulders as they walked.

There was a crowd of noisy backpackers drinking on the shore, so they moved far away, until they found an isolated spot. They sat hand in hand looking out at the moonlit water.

"When I've finished my book, we should go away together somewhere, even just for a few days," June said.

"I'd love that. You know what else I'd love to do?"

"What's that?" June asked.

"I want to introduce you to my folks."

June bumped Trish with her shoulder. "Wow, I know people joke about lesbians moving fast but you're not playing around, are you?"

Trish laughed. "Hey. I meant when we're ready. You already know Leigh. You can come to one of our family dinners. I'd love to meet your mother too. Do you think she'd cook me dinner sometime?"

"I think she'd love to cook for you," June said, squeezing her hand.

They took turns sharing plans and ideas. Trish listened as June's voice hummed quietly in the night. This would be a part of her life now, the indescribable happiness of being at June's side.

As June spoke, Trish promised herself that she would live up to the faith June was placing in her. No matter what, Trish was going to do her best to make sure that her insecurities and doubts never led her around by the nose again.

Trish was still going to do all the things that she wanted to do before this miracle had occurred. It was unfair to expect June to be everything for her. After Katrina, she couldn't risk making the same mistake of allowing one person to rule her life so completely. Trish wanted to take command of her own fate, and she wanted to be able to come home to June every night and share it with her. Trish was sure that such an arrangement would be the only one that June could be happy with, and that was why she was special.

It was too soon to say *I love you* but Trish was sure that she did. She wanted to know that June felt the same way, but for now it was enough to have her here. Maybe one day soon June would tell her, and that was something to look forward to.

"What are you thinking about, looking all serious like that? I can barely see your face, but I know you look serious," June said.

"Nothing at all. Everything is perfect," Trish said.

They finished eating from their cartons. Abruptly, June pulled the blanket from their shoulders and laid it down on the sand, standing up to smooth it over the ground. She beckoned Trish forward and they lay down together.

Trish looked up at the stars for a moment. This moment really was perfect. She closed her eyes.

June was propped on her elbow beside her. Trish looked up at her and slipped a hand around her neck. They kissed, the spark igniting quickly between them again.

It was late, and there was nobody else on the beach. Trish looked up and around them to be certain, then she slowly pushed up June's shirt. She found the skin warm beneath her hand, and as they kissed, she laid a hand over June's chest to feel her quickening breath.

They made love while the waves lapped at the shore.

CHAPTER TWENTY

Trish sipped her wine and made small talk with one of the groomsmen sitting next to her. Bobby was Andrew's colleague and one of his best friends. Throughout the time leading up to the wedding, Trish had spent quite a lot of time with him.

"Your girlfriend seems really cool. What's her name again?" Bobby said.

"June," Trish said absently, because at every opportunity she had been taking in the sight of June dressed in a well-tailored, very flattering black suit. The pants gathered in at the ankle and she was wearing heels, with her hair flowing loosely. As usual, June's androgynous beauty drove her crazy. Judging from the stares June had been getting all night from even the heterosexual women in the room, Trish was not the only one who felt that way.

The wedding was beautiful, and the reception was shaping up to be great too. Both events were held at a winery in the Yarra Valley. Though it was now dark, they had been surrounded all day by stunning mountain views. It was one of the first days of summer, and a shining sun blessed them all afternoon.

The reception hall was an old mansion, with polished floorboards and stunning antique furniture. Andrew and Leigh had chosen brightly colored floral centerpieces for the tables, and the room was lit with lanterns that cast a soft glow over the room.

Many of the guests were drunk, thanks to the countless toasts that had been proposed during the speeches. Trish and Leigh's dad had brought the room to tears as he talked about his daughter. Now the band was playing a mixture of eighties-era covers and sappy ballads, and people were dancing.

The only problem was that Trish was seated at the bridal table at the top end of the room, where they looked out over all the guests, and therefore she couldn't sit next to June. They had spent the last few nights apart because Trish had been so busy with her bridesmaids' duties. Of course, Trish was happy to do it, even if having a man for a partner all night made her feel like she was back at one of her high school dances. Bobby was a good guy, so it wasn't as painful as it could have been to have a whole night on his arm.

June seemed to be getting along well without her. Trish watched June pull a chair out for one of her great-aunts. It was the first time June had met most of her extended family, and she was charming all of them. At one point, Trish looked up to find a few of her cousins, together with a handful of aunts and uncles, crowded around June. They were all smiling and laughing, and Trish watched proudly as June held them in her thrall. She would have to ask later what they were all talking about.

Trish had already introduced June to her parents, who got over their fixation on Katrina right away. June had come to two family dinners in a row, so that she met their dad one week and their mother the following. Trish was so relieved at the way June talked with her mom about books when they first met, discussing her mother's passion for Gloria Steinem and Susan Sontag. Then June spent hours discussing food and wine with her dad, debating which region produced the best shiraz, and where the best blue cheese could be found.

Trish had met June's family, too, and had gotten along well with June's mother, Gwen. Gwen was younger than her own parents, and dressed stylishly in vintage clothing from Fitzroy boutiques. Trish found her to be warm and funny, just the kind of person that she would have imagined raising June. It was fascinating to learn about June's early years, how Gwen had managed working as a chef in tourist traps throughout Northern Queensland when June was a baby.

As Trish watched June talking to her relatives, June looked back over at her. They stared at one another for a moment, losing focus on the conversations they'd been having. June lifted her hands and used her fingers and thumbs to make a heart sign.

"Should we go out and dance?" Bobby asked.

"Of course," Trish said.

Trish had shed her heels a while ago because they had been giving her a headache, so she went out to the dance floor with bare feet. A lot of the men had loosened their ties and taken off their jackets.

While they danced, Trish looked over Bobby's shoulder at Leigh and Andrew, who were moving while they stared into one another's eyes. Trish had cried tears of happiness during their vows, so thrilled for her big sister. The newlyweds were going overseas for a month-long honeymoon, and Trish was going to miss Leigh like crazy.

Bobby spun Trish around, placing June directly in her line of sight. June was dancing with Trish's cousin Shane, and she did not like the way that he was looking at June. Trish rolled her eyes. Shane had always been sleazy.

Trish realized that Bobby was looking at her face, noting that she was paying no attention to him at all.

"You know you can go and dance with her! My wife would be pleased to have me back for a dance or two," he said.

"We can do that now, can't we?" Trish said.

"Of course we can. I think the duty part of the night is pretty much over. Why don't you go and get your girl and I'll go get mine?"

Trish agreed, and they shook on it, grinning at one another. She approached her cousin and stood behind his shoulder, tapping him on the fabric of his ugly suit.

"Mind if I cut in?"

Shane looked back at her sheepishly, stepping away from June. Trish moved close to June, putting her hands behind June's neck whilst June touched her waist.

"Can I tell you again that you look amazing in that suit?"

"You can tell me as many times as you like. I'm just happy you're here, I was hoping I'd get my hands on that hot bridesmaid I've had my eye on all night," June said, smirking.

"Well good, but I felt like you needed a rescue from octopus hands. He didn't try anything, did he?"

"Oh, he's fine, I've handled much worse than him at the bar."

They'd discovered a while ago that June loved to dance and that Trish had no idea how, so they'd been working on their moves in preparation for tonight. There had been many evenings of dancing around the living room at Trish's place. They played all their favorite songs, listening to Stax and Motown tracks while they danced for hours.

Now they gently swayed back and forth to a cheesy Bryan Adams song, their bodies fitting together perfectly.

"See, you don't have two left feet," June said softly, close to her ear.

"I'm managing okay, right? "

"You're managing it perfectly, baby."

Trish burrowed into the crook of June's neck, smelling her hair and the delicious scent of her skin. June's hands were around Trish's waist, holding her tight. The thrill of June's touch had not faded a bit over the past few months.

"You looked so great up there today," June said. "And I loved your speech."

"Do you really think so? I still don't think it was as good as some of the others," Trish said.

Trish had fretted over it for weeks, writing countless drafts and constantly seeking out June's opinion to make sure that she didn't forget anything.

"Stop it," June said gently. "Believe me, it was amazing. You should be proud."

Trish nodded and leaned in closer, allowing herself to feel the calm that washed over her with June's presence. Since they'd been together she'd stopped worrying quite as much, trying to follow June's lead and be less rigid about the little things. It was a lot of work sometimes, but she could honestly say that she was becoming a happier person.

June's breath brushed against her cheek. "And your dress looks perfect on you, by the way. You are so pretty."

Trish pulled back and looked into her eyes, enjoying the silent understanding between them.

"Can you two please not upstage me at my own wedding?" Leigh called out as she and Andrew danced past them. They drew a little bit closer and Leigh cupped a hand around her mouth. "You're being obscene, you look like you're going to start banging one another up here."

Trish shook her head, scowling at Leigh's back as Andrew turned her away.

"She's so crude," Trish muttered.

"She's just teasing you."

Trish knew she was right. Nobody had been happier for the two of them than her sister was. They had all hung out as a group regularly, often having dinner at Andrew and Leigh's place. There had been many nights during which they'd gone to June's bar for free drinks, waiting for her to finish work so they could all go out together afterward.

"C'mon, I want to sneak out of here and have a cigarette," Leigh said as they started to leave the dance floor. "I need you girls to help me."

"Okay, let's pretend we're helping you to the bathroom," Trish said. Making sure Leigh could go to the bathroom without spoiling the long train on her dress had been one of the most challenging parts of her day.

They managed to get outside without too much interference from guests, finding a quiet spot on the wooden porch of the rustic brick building. Leigh leaned up against the wall and pulled a cigarette and lighter from her cleavage, looking like she was in heaven as she sparked up the flame.

"I didn't even know you smoked," June said.

"She doesn't. Or, hasn't for years, anyway, after I begged her to quit. Where did you get that from?"

"Uncle Alex. I totally deserve the stress relief. Why doesn't anyone ever tell you weddings are a goddamn nightmare?"

They spoke quietly to avoid drawing attention to themselves, going over the day. The drumbeat in the music was a dull thud through the wall.

"It's nearly time for Andrew and me to do the big exit. You'll look after my little sister while I'm overseas, won't you, June?"

June grabbed Trish's hand. "She doesn't need any looking after, but I will anyway."

"Good."

Trish and June gazed at one another in the near-dark, oblivious to the fact that Leigh was watching them.

"Which one of you girls is going to catch the bouquet?"

"No offense, but I'm not going to do that. Not really my thing."

"June, June, June. You're a part of this family now, and in case you can't tell, this family digs weddings. You'll never be truly accepted unless you do shit like scramble for that bouquet alongside Aunt Theresa."

"We'll see," June replied.

They switched the lights on as they entered their hotel room, and June laid the bouquet down on one of the nightstands. It had been an epic battle against Trish's aunt, but June had won it fair and square.

She kicked off her heels and rubbed her feet. She was happy to wear heels when the occasion called for it, but right now she wished she'd stuck to her boots.

Trish stretched and turned around. "Can you unzip me?"

June went to Trish and slowly drew the zip down her back. The dress really was gorgeous on her, the shape of it perfect for her slim waist and elegant back. June kissed the exposed skin of that back, and moved up to Trish's neck.

June assumed that Trish would be too tired to have sex tonight. Though being apart for the last few nights had built up an aching need, June understood that she would have to wait at least one more. She was pleasantly surprised when Trish turned in her arms and reached for her like she had so many times before.

They made love slowly, on the soft hotel sheets, moving against one another in the dark. Just when she was certain that she couldn't feel any closer to Trish, and that it couldn't be any better than it already was, it would change. They had spent so many hours learning about one another's bodies, discovering what the other liked. June loved staying in bed with Trish for hours, talking and making love, then doing it all over again.

"I'm too wired to go to sleep," Trish said.

June held her from behind. The sheet was draped across their bodies, the bed soft and cushiony. She was the same, tired but not sleepy.

"I know what you mean."

"It really was a beautiful day. They all loved you."

"I had a great time. Your family's awesome."

"I was so proud to introduce you to everyone." June kissed Trish's temple, brushing her hand over Trish's shoulder. "I love you."

They had said it to one another a month or so into their relationship. June had held back, trying to wait until Trish said it first. She had been sure of her own feelings for a while but hadn't wanted to rush anything. One night, when they had been lying just like this, it slipped from her lips as she was going to sleep. June awoke to find Trish waiting for her, eager to return the words. After that they held one another so tightly June felt like her heart was going to burst.

"I love you too."

"Weddings make you think about stuff, don't they?" Trish said.

"They do make you think about…stuff…" June said.

"What are you thinking about?"

June rolled over and raised her eyebrows. "You're cheating. You say it first."

"Well, you know. That it might be nice to do something like that one day."

"This is a really shitty proposal."

"I'm sorry," Trish said, clasping June's hand. "I don't think either of us are ready for that right now. Right?"

"I'm just teasing you. Of course, I thought about it too. Go on, what did you want to say?"

"I'd like to take the next step."

"You want to move in together?" June said.

"I do. What do you think?"

"I do too," June said, pulling Trish close for a hug. "How? I'm guessing you don't want to live with Ollie and me. So, I'd move into your place?"

"No. It's where I lived with Katrina. I hate that house. I want to sell it. I'll sell it, and we'll get a place to rent for a while. I don't know what I'm waiting for."

"And when I'm making more money we can get our own place maybe?" June said.

"Exactly."

They sealed the plan with a kiss.

June felt lighter just thinking about it. There would be no more spending nights apart. There would be only Sunday mornings and crawling into bed with one another late at night, sharing their days, cooking, cleaning, being together. They would fight over who should clean the bathroom and make up because it didn't really matter. There would be a study for June and a porch where they would have their breakfast.

"Well, this is exciting. I feel like getting out of bed to start working on the plans right now. It's going to be amazing to get the place sold. I can't wait. I should find an agent."

"Don't get out of bed now, baby. There's always tomorrow," June murmured.

As June slipped into sleep she could see it all laid out before them. All the mornings and nights, and everything in between flashed in her mind in an instant. It was a book that she wanted so badly to write, and she already knew the ending.

Bella Books, Inc.

Women. Books. Even Better Together.

P.O. Box 10543
Tallahassee, FL 32302

Phone: 800-729-4992
www.bellabooks.com